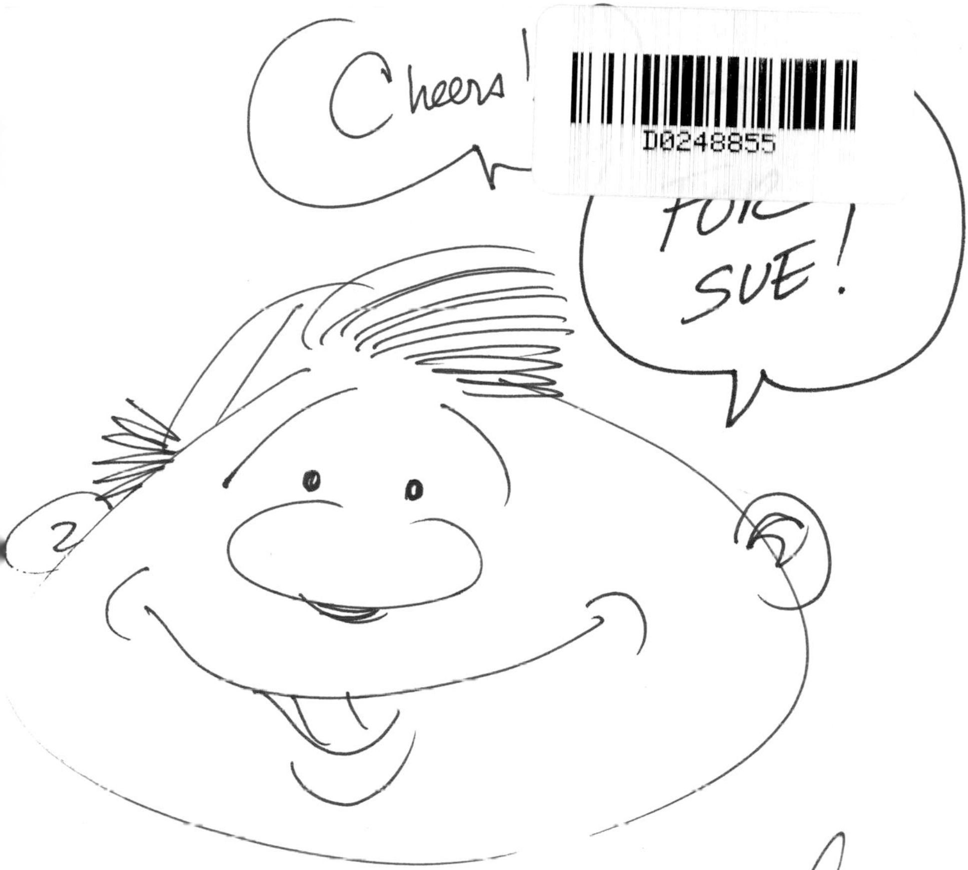

from William J. Nolan
June 19. '99

THE BLACK MASK MURDERS

Other Fiction by William F. Nolan

Night Shapes

Helle on Wheels

3 for Space

Helltracks

Blood Sky

Rio Renegades

Logan: A Trilogy

Look Out for Space

Things Beyond Midnight

Logan's Search

Logan's World

Wonderworlds

Alien Horizons

Space for Hire

The White Cad Cross-up

Death Is for Losers

Logan's Run

Impact 20

William F. Nolan

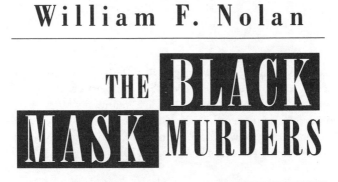

THE BLACK MASK MURDERS

*A Novel Featuring
The Black Mask Boys:*

DASHIELL HAMMETT,

RAYMOND CHANDLER,

AND

ERLE STANLEY GARDNER

ST. MARTIN'S PRESS   NEW YORK

Design by Basha Zapatka

LIBRARY OF CONGRESS CATALOGING IN PUBLICATION DATA

Nolan, William F.
   The black mask murders/William F. Nolan.
      p.   cm.
   "A Thomas Dunne book."
   ISBN 0-312-10942-3
   1. Gardner, Erle Stanley, 1889-1970—Fiction.   2. Hammett, Dashiell,—1894-1961—Fiction.   3. Chandler, Raymond, 1888-1959—Fiction.   4. Authors, American—20th century—Fiction.   5. Murder—California—Fiction.   I. Title.
PS3564.O39B58   1994
813'.54—dc20   94–603

First Edition: July 1994
10 9 8 7 6 5 4 3 2 1

For my oldest friend,
WILLIAM J. HENNESSEY,
who shared the Kansas City years.

A thousand memories, Bill!

ONE

A Friday afternoon in late October. Dim and gusty. Halloween weather. The soot-colored sky was packed with swollen gray clouds fat as dirigibles. The radio said we'd have rain tomorrow from a storm blowing in off the Pacific, a sub-tropical downpour, the kind Los Angeles specializes in.

Rain doesn't bother me. Makes everything shiny and new, scours off all the caked-dry desert dust, and I like the fresh clean smell of it. After a Los Angeles rain, the air is full of honeysuckle and pine. Makes me think of summer days when I was a kid back in Maryland and I'd sit on the bank of the Patuxent and watch the rain slash down, cutting into the surface of the river like tiny silver knives. Those were good, easy days. Southern days. All I had to think about was the moment at hand. Becoming an adult with adult problems was impossible to imagine, a million years away.

Of course, that was when I was very young. It hadn't lasted long; I was forced to grow up fast. My father was a rigid, severe man with questionable morals, and my mother was never quite comfortable in the world as it existed. Aloof and dreaming, her mind was fixed on our French ancestors and the fantasy life she

1

was sure they'd enjoyed. I had to quit school at fourteen, and I've been on my own ever since.

Damn! Why was I dredging up all this stuff from the past? Anything to keep from writing, eh, Hammett?

I turned away from the gray cloud mass outside my office window and rolled another sheet of paper into my gleaming studio typewriter. Fancy machine. Some German brand I couldn't pronounce, imported by Global Studios. I preferred working on my Smith Corona Super-Speed—I wrote *The Thin Man* on it—but the studio would never have approved. Global's writers were supposed to use the latest equipment, and for what I was getting paid, I wasn't about to rock any boats. Last year, in '34, I pulled in eighty grand (thanks in large part to M-G-M), and this year was ever better. Hotcha! The long green had my name on it and life was plush. The Great Depression wasn't touching us here in Hollywood; we all lived in our own golden bubble, and that suited me fine.

I'd been hired to create a screen scenario for the reigning queen of Global, Sylvia Vane. Sultry Sylvia, the slithering siren of sex. With those big, long-lashed bedroom eyes and a figure with more curves in it than Sunset Boulevard. The public couldn't get enough of her; women lusted after her seductive secrets, and the men just lusted. Her pictures were box office dynamite: *Arabian Love Slave, Flame of Desire, Pits of Passion, The Devil's Playground*—all produced so they didn't actually transgress the written standards of the officious prudes at the Hays Office. Global was expert in twisting the censorship regulations so its films were approved, but just barely. And it was the "just barely" that had catapulted Global to the top.

But Sylvia got ambitious. She wanted to be considered a *serious* actress, another Garbo. So she told Ernie Bulow, who owns Global, that her talent was not being exercised and she needed to stretch her creative muscles. Ernie blew his top, but Sylvia

2

was adamant. She demanded a change of pace, a "totally new" kind of role to sink her dramatic teeth into. No more panting sex sirens in feather boas and low-cut evening gowns (who, in keeping with the Hays Code, inevitably paid for their scarlet sins at the end of each film). She informed Ernie that she wanted a role with "class." She wanted to play a sexy gangster's moll. Don't ask me how a sexy gangster's moll adds up to "class." Who can figure actresses?

Which is where I come in. Right away, Ernie Bulow thought of me. I'd built a rep for this sort of thing. At Paramount they'd hired me to develop a gangland saga for Gary Cooper, *City Streets*. Coop loved it and so did the studio. (I'd gambled away my five grand bonus for that one in an all-night poker game with Ben Hecht.) And for Zanuck, at Warners, I'd written *Private Detective*—about a seedy private eye involved in the New York rackets. My *Glass Key* was now in release, featuring real life tough guy George Raft, and there was my hotsy *Thin Man* series starring Bill Powell for M-G-M. When the movie moguls wanted a slick gangster story whomped up for the silver screen, Hammett was their boy.

God knows, my stuff is authentic enough. During my years as a national operative for Pinkerton I worked the full range of crime, from petty theft to murder. I'd exposed counterfeiters, investigated bank swindlers, trapped blackmailers, trailed jewel thieves, uncovered missing gold shipments, arrested forgers, tangled with gangsters and holdup men, gathered evidence for criminal trials, and performed services as bodyguard, hotel detective, and strikebreaker.

But all that was over, and so here I was at Global, sitting in front of a German typewriter in my office on a gloomy Friday in October, trying like hell to finish the last twenty pages of script I needed to wrap up *Blood Roads*. Sylvia Vane would star as an orphan girl from Kansas City who hooks up with John Dillinger's gang as his number one blonde floozie. We weren't actually calling our guy Dillinger, because the real John D. was supposedly shot to death in Chicago last year in front of the Biograph Theater. (Personally, I don't buy it. I figure he's still on the lam and that the gundown in Chi was a setup between Dillinger and some crooked Indiana cops, and that a pigeon named Jimmy Lawrence is the one they buried—but that's another story.)

In *Blood Roads* our gangster was "Johnny Dodge"—but I had him robbing the same banks Dillinger had robbed, and I used Dillinger's escape from the Crown Point jail (where he carved a gun from a stick of wood) as one of my key scenes. Johnny is wounded after an armored car job goes sour in Kansas and the G-men close in. Sylvia thinks he's dying and she rocks him in her arms like a baby. I made sure there was plenty of ham in the scene for dear Sylvia. She loves to sob onscreen and I knew she'd have a field day with this. Guaranteed schmaltz.

So, okay, fine. I had my big scene but I was twenty pages short of winding up the script and nothing I'd written so far was any damn good. All hack junk. My wastebasket was full of lousy pages.

I needed a cigarette to help me think, but after Erle Gardner kept ragging me about how smoking dulls your senses and ruins your heart and cuts down your sexual endurance, I'd quit cold. It was the sexual endurance part that got to me. So I munched on a pencil instead. I'd chewed my way through four Ticonderogas when someone rapped sharply on my office door.

"Dash! Goddammit, are you *in* there?" A woman's voice that I recognized instantly. Sultry Sylvia. The cinema queen herself.

"It's open," I told her.

She swept in. Understand, Sylvia didn't *walk* into a room, she swept into it. And she never *sat* on couches, she draped herself over them. That's what she did on mine. Silk whispered on silk as she crossed her long legs. She was wearing a casual little

4

afternoon frock that would set back the average secretary two years pay. Her handbag and pumps were trimmed in antique gold and they matched the tony Tiffany circlet around her celebrated swanlike throat.

"Got a cigarette?" she asked, looking at me with her big, long-lashed siren's eyes.

"Gave 'em up. I chew pencils instead. I can offer you a fresh Ticonderoga."

"I hate people who give up things," she said. Her voice changed, dropped to rich velvet. "Excess," she intoned softly. "That's the real secret of living. Give me a man who is not afraid of his passions, who tears the heart out of life."

"*Devil's Playground*," I said. "Scene just before you seduce the gypsy's brother."

She broke into hard laughter. Tallulah Bankhead laughs like that, a harsh grating sound. "Damn you, Hammett! I can't vamp you for sour apples!"

"Oh, sure you can. I'm a pushover for a slim ankle and a sucker for a wet kiss." I grinned. "But you're not here to seduce me."

"No," she said, "not really."

"And you're not here to ask me how the script is coming."

"No, I'm not."

"Then why *are* you here?"

She leaned forward on the couch, her eyes suddenly intense. "Dash . . . I'm in big trouble."

"What kind of trouble?"

"Gambling trouble."

"Meaning you've been losing and you owe somebody a lot of money."

"Tony Richetti," she said. The velvet was gone; her voice was almost shrill.

"How much?"

"Over fifty thousand."

"Faro? Roulette? Craps?"

"Roulette."

I shifted back in my chair. "Been going out to the *Lady*, eh?"

"Every weekend. That ship's been a curse! Even my salary for this picture is gone. Ernie paid me in advance when I told him I needed the money."

She dipped into her purse and passed me a note. Handwritten in midnight blue ink on custom ivory paperstock as thick as clotted cream.

Pay what you owe me or
suffer the consequences.

It was signed with a sprawling *R. Richetti*.

"He's not kidding," she said. "About the consequences. I've heard what Tony's done to people who don't pay him. They end up in a hospital. If they're lucky."

"I'm sorry," I said, handing back the note. "But what can I do about it?"

"Find out if his wheels are rigged. You're an experienced gambler. You can find out if Tony's using a brake."

"I'm out of it, Sylvia," I told her. "Gamblers never win. That's the title of a mystery I read once in Baltimore. It's still true. That's why I quit. It's a fool's game."

"You've never been aboard the *Lady*?"

"Never. Too damn tempting."

"Look," she said, standing up and walking toward me, "I'm not asking you to start gambling again. I'm just asking you to find out if Tony's running a crooked wheel."

"And what if he is? You'll still owe him the fifty gees. And the law boys won't help. Richetti's operating beyond the three-mile limit. The cops can't touch him."

"I'm not thinking about the police," she said. "If I was *certain* Tony's been cheating me . . . if you could prove it . . . then I'd make a deal with him."

"Richetti doesn't make deals with anybody."

"He will with me if I have the goods on him. Deal is, he forgets what I owe him and I don't spill the beans to his customers. I know a lot of people in this town. If they ever find out the action is dirty on board the *Lady* they'll switch to *The Lucky Horseshoe* and Big Bill Kelly will get all the play. Tony will be out of business."

"So I'm the guy you've come to for a bailout?"

"Because I know you can do it. You can get me the proof I need."

"And what do *I* get out of it?"

She was sitting on the edge of my desk, letting one leg swing slowly, seductively. She licked her full lips, red as firetrucks. "Me," she said.

I thought that one over. We'd kidded around some, but I never figured to end up between Sylvia Vane's silk sheets.

It was a nice thought. And it kept getting nicer.

"Well . . . what do you say, Dash?" Her look was languid.

"I say sure. Okay. I'll do it."

She reached over the desk, gave me a soft kiss on the cheek, and slithered out of my office, leaving behind the scent of her very expensive French perfume to remind me of how big a sap I am for beautiful women.

TWO

I left the studio in my chauffeured limousine. I don't drive—and there's a reason. I was in the army once and I got assigned to the Motor Ambulance Company at Camp Meade, in Maryland, as a transport driver. But I was never any good behind the wheel and I hated manhandling those big, clumsy, top-heavy machines. The roads were lousy, just ridged dirt full of rocks and potholes. I was transporting a load of patients to the hospital one morning when I hit a half-buried rock and the whole shebang went ass over teakettle. The road was filled with groaning patients, but luckily nobody was killed. I shattered an elbow and never drove again. In or out of the army.

A limo is wonderful. You just sit back and relax on that soft leather seat and let the driver do all the work. My chauffeur is a lanky guy from Haiti named Leonce Lebert Aurele Desvarieux. I call him "Buddy" because I can never remember his real name. He always calls me "Chief." He understands the crummy moods I get into from time to time. Thing is, I was trying to finish another novel for Knopf. I had a title, *There Was a Young Man*, and a plan for the book. It was going to be about the years when I was an operative for Pinkerton's National Detective Agency.

Not the kind of wild melodrama I wrote for Joe Shaw in *Black Mask*. This book would be the genuine goods, the way it really was. But I didn't get much done on it because big-bucks studio jobs kept getting in the way. One thing was certain—I wasn't going to get sucked back into writing for *Mask*. Shaw was sending me these tear-stained letters telling me how his readers kept asking when I would return with another Continental Op story and I kept writing back to say Never is when. Never. But Joe's stubborn; he doesn't take No for an answer.

Ray Chandler picked up with *Mask* where I left off, and Erle Gardner is still churning out four or five of his Phantom Crook novelettes each year for Joe, even though his Perry Mason character is taking off. Warners has done three Masons just this year, so Erle knows he has a tiger by the tail. Chandler keeps talking about trying a novel, but he can't seem to get past the shorter stuff. He's always been a slow worker and novels can take a while. With Ray, you don't push. You suggest, you advise, but you don't push.

My novels aren't such hot stuff. I don't think much of them. *The Glass Key* and *The Maltese Falcon* are okay, but *Red Harvest* is too damn bloody and *The Dain Curse* is crap. Just silly crap. That's when I was trying to be Gothic! Jeez! I hear that Hemingway liked *Curse*, but he's nuts. That *Farewell to Arms* of his is full of sappy love scenes that could never happen between a real soldier and his nurse. Some of the war stuff is good, but Hemingway just can't write women. Gertie Stein told him that once, and she should know when it comes to women. I like *The Thin Man* best because it's earned me the most money. It's like a slot that just keeps spilling out jackpots. That's a good reason to like a book.

I know my best novel is still ahead of me if I can get myself settled into it. Maybe in nineteen hundred thirty-six. Yeah, next year for sure. I'll make it my New Year's resolution.

Buddy drove me home. To the Harold Lloyd house in Pacific Palisades just beyond Brentwood, a cozy little 44-room mansion I'd leased on M-G-M's money. Huge pool. Gardens chock-full of palm trees and California's bright-colored flowers. And with a tennis court big enough to stage the Indy 500. A great joint for parties.

I have a weakness for strawberry double-dip sodas, so I had M-G-M install an ice cream fountain in the rumpus room. There were chicken sandwiches in the refrigerator, enough for Buddy and me. We were hungry. Finished off the sandwiches with some vanilla ice cream from C.C. Brown's. Everybody raves about Brown's hot fudge sundaes, but I've always liked their vanilla ice cream best.

Buddy wanted to know if I'd be needing him later and I said yes, by ten-thirty. That's when I planned to go out to Richetti's gambling ship and mingle with the swells. The action starts to get heavy around midnight and I'd have a good chance to look things over without attracting too much attention.

The phone rang. It was John Daly, calling from his home in White Plains, New York. His full name is Carroll John Daly, but nobody calls him Carroll except his mother. He's a hack writer in the worst sense of the term, but he has the dubious distinction of having created the world's first full-blown private eye, Race Williams, in the pages of *Black Mask* back in '23. This was just before my first Continental Op yarn was printed there that same year. John's stuff was terrible right from the start, and it's never gotten any better. His dialogue is impossibly stilted and his style is a direct carryover from the lurid blood-and-thunder dime novels of earlier, less sophisticated times.

Race Williams is a ridiculous gun-crazed vigilante who enjoys pumping bullets into anyone who gets in his way. John himself is a shy, wispy little guy who has never fired a gun in his life. He's terrified of having his teeth fixed, for God's sake, and he seldom ventures beyond the confines of his own front yard.

When John tried to involve Race in a romance with a female crook he called "The Flame," his style reached a new low. Word for awful word, here's how The Flame attempts to seduce Williams:

> Oh, I used men . . . My mind guided me—that criminal mind. There's never been a man who held me in his arms and kissed me who hasn't come back and back and back. Moths! Moths! Moths to The Flame! Race, I can offer you power. I can take the world's greatest racket and lay it at your feet. Me—a slip of a girl—The Flame . . . I want you! I love you! Oh, Race! Race! . . .

And it goes on like that.

When Joe Shaw took over the editor's chair at *Mask* he intended to get rid of Race Williams, but the readers wouldn't let him. For years he was forced to keep printing what he called "this mindless drip." Shaw was finally able to ease Williams out of the magazine in '34. John hasn't been able to sell Joe Shaw a word over the past year. In fact, that was what his call was about.

"Dash, I know you carry a lot of weight with Shaw. He listens to what you tell him. I need your help."

"To do what?"

"To get Race back into *Black Mask*. My God, I was one of the stars! When my name was on the cover there was always a big jump in sales. Then, suddenly, I'm out! Why does Shaw hate me?"

"Nobody hates you, John," I told him. "You're a nice guy and Joe has never said a word against you personally. It's just that he doesn't like what you write."

"But I'm a pioneer! I'm the father of the hard-boiled detective!"

11

"True enough, John, but that doesn't change the way Shaw feels about your stuff."

His voice was a whine. "All I'm asking, Dash, as a personal favor from one colleague to another, is for you to tell Shaw that you'd like to see Race back in the *Mask*."

"You know I can't do that, John. I'm sorry, but my opinion of what you write won't allow it."

"I've improved! I'm *much* better now."

"I saw some of your recent stuff in *Dime Detective* and I'm afraid I can't agree."

Now his tone was low and defeated. "Then you refuse to talk to Shaw?"

"Joe knows how I feel. I'd be playing it phony and I just can't do that."

"Then I'll tell you want you *can* do, Dash," he said, his tone now edged and shrill. "You can go straight to hell!"

And that ended our conversation.

I sat there for a long moment with the dead phone in my hand, feeling like a louse. But the fact was, Daly had no right to ask me to lie to Joe Shaw. Knowing that, however, didn't make me feel any better.

I had some time to kill. Jack Benny was doing a guest stint with Louella Parsons on *Hollywood Hotel*, and I always enjoyed Benny's off-key violin playing, but I didn't feel like a radio show. What I felt like was a nap.

The master bedroom reminded me of how much money Harold Lloyd had made falling off buildings. Looked like something you'd see in a Busby Berkeley musical, with enough room for fifty dancing girls and a brass band.

I flopped onto the Louis Quatorze bed, setting my alarm clock for nine-thirty. Which would give me time to get up, shave the day's stubble off my chin, shower, and slip into the tux I'd borrowed from Global's costume department. Studio tuxedos are tailored better. They have to be. Fred Astaire had danced in this one.

The second I hit the mattress I was out and I slept like an innocent babe until the alarm went off.

I felt great. Full of energy.

I'd need it before the night was over.

Buddy dropped me off at the Santa Monica pier. Full of Friday night noise. A wash of tinny music from the Penny Arcade competed with the frog-throated barkers hawking peep shows. The aroma of hot buttered popcorn reminded me of all the movies Pop would never let me go to. The other kids were handed shiny nickels for their admission tickets, but if I wanted to see a film I had to sneak into the theater. When I got caught, which was about once a month, Pop would come down on me for wasting my mind. Maybe the movies *were* pretty crude in those early days, but there was an aura of excitement about them. The stage never interested me the way movies did, but I've changed a lot since then. The stage is *immediate*. It plays to your gut. Last year I worked with Lily—that's Lillian Hellman—on *The Children's Hour*, which opened on Broadway in November. Big hit. Lily's a natural playwright and I predict she's going to be great once she gets rolling.

At the end of the pier, I walked past a bingo parlor full of rheumy-eyed oldsters, looking for the water taxi that would take me out to the *Lady*. Over the phone they'd told me another was due to leave at eleven-thirty, and it was close to that now.

Then I saw the bright yellow glass-topped motor launch easing into its berth at the pier's edge.

That Pacific storm the radio talked about had obviously blown itself out before it hit the coast and the wind had died down. Beyond the breakers, the water was calm, with a light fog curling in. The pier smelled of brine and kelp and the waves kept spilling their white lace against dark pilings.

Three other potential gamblers were making the trip. A robust middle-aged woman in furs, who wore too much lip rouge, was hanging onto the arms of two younger male companions in well-cut evening clothes. She was giggling as they helped her down the steep wooden steps into the idling water taxi. Her two friends exchanged a look that said, what the hell, she's paying so let's enjoy it.

The ride out cost a quarter and took thirty minutes. As we rounded the stone breakwater into open sea, the fog closed in, ghost-white against our running lights. Then it thinned again as we got farther out and I could see the illuminated bulk of Richetti's big gambling ship rising from the water. She was lit like a dozen Christmas trees and her music drifted out to us, a siren call in the night. My fingers itched; I could feel the snap of playing cards in my hands, sense the carnival click of a turning roulette wheel, feel the green baize of a faro table under my palms.

The old fever—all over again.

Now, through the misting fog, the ship was in close sight ahead of us. On her bow, in glowing neon: *The Wicked Lady*. She rode steady in the oil-black sea, anchored by four thick hawsers. A searchlight from the upper deck flared over us; then the bright beam swept away as we passed the two stern hawsers to reach the landing stage. The taximan throttled back his engine, the burbling sound of the exhaust drowned by a tide of festive music from the ship.

The lady in furs, still giggling, and her two bored companions were helped onto the bright-lit landing stage. I followed them aboard, looking snappy in Fred Astaire's tuxedo but feeling tense, the way I felt in the old Pinkerton days when I was heading into possible gunplay. Gambling is an addiction, and right then it was running my blood. Up to now, I'd been wise to stay away from the *Lady*. But at least I'd done one smart thing: I'd left all my money behind except for two hundred bucks, which I could easily afford to lose. There wouldn't be any thousand dollar wagers against the house on this trip. (Early last year at the Clover Club in Hollywood, with Lily in attendance, I'd lost $19,000 in one night at chemin de fer. I hadn't gambled since.)

The gaming salon was below the boat deck. That's where all the action was. I walked past the glittering cabaret on the upper level and down a wide red-carpet stairway to the gambling area. The brightness made me dizzy when I stepped through a curtained archway into the main salon; you couldn't get more light out of the sun at high noon. The place was jammed. Noisy. Smoky. Exciting. Yeah, to me, exciting. I could feel my heart beating hard against my chest.

There was a familiar odor in the air: the smell of desperation. Losers were giving way to panic; beneath their custom-tailored dinner jackets and swank evening gowns a fear sweat beaded their skin. And, as always, there were plenty of losers.

A Negro quartet was putting out some sweet jazz on a raised bandstand at the far end of the salon, but nobody was paying much attention. The music they listened to was the snap of cards on green-felt tables, the rattle of dice in a cup, the click of a turning roulette wheel.

I spotted three wheels, all well attended, and drifted toward the nearest to observe the action. The flat, emotionless voice of the croupier was droning, "Place your bets, ladies and gentlemen. Place your bets." Rainbow-hued chips were stacked on squared numbers. The wheel spun and the little ivory ball began its jittery dance. A money dance. Every eye was locked on it.

"Dash! Well, by *God!*" A hand touched my shoulder and I turned to a man behind me. He was smiling broadly.

"Scotty," I said, acknowledging him with a smile of my own.

I shook hands with F. Scott Fitzgerald. I hadn't seen him in two years, since we'd worked on a musical together for RKO. I wasn't any good at musicals, which was why they'd brought in Scotty—but he stayed drunk for the entire six weeks we were on the script so they fired both of us.

"Somebody told me you gave up this vice," Fitzgerald said. He had very thin lips and delicate features, with a face right out of the flapper era he got famous for writing about.

"Then somebody told you wrong," I said. I used Sylvia's line: "I hate people who give up things."

"My luck's gone sour," Scotty told me. "Remember that diamond watch I bought Zelda for our wedding anniversary?"

"Yeah," I nodded. "A beaut."

"I hocked it to get out here tonight. But I've had the damndest luck. Just the damndest."

I shrugged. "That's the way it goes sometimes." I wondered how things were going for Zelda. I'd heard some dark rumors about her mental condition. Were they true? I was afraid to ask.

"I'm heading up to the cabaret for a bracer," said Fitzgerald. "Care to join me? I've got enough dough left for a couple of dry martinis."

"Sorry. Just got here. I have some money to lose."

"Well, I hope you don't. Lose, that is. I *hate* to lose." He grinned. "Guess everybody does, eh?" He shook my hand again. "Been great seeing you, Dash. Maybe another time?"

"Sure, Scotty," I said. "Another time."

I turned back to the wheel, thinking about the poor bastard. All that talent—and all that booze. A bad combination. Most writers drink. I do. Ray Chandler does. Lily does. But we try to keep it at a social level. No week-long binges. No gin bottles at ten in the morning.

I reminded myself that I was here to do a job, not worry about hopeless drunks like Fitzgerald. Sylvia was depending on me.

16

A good wheelman can use a brake so effectively you just can't spot his action. He can make that bouncing ivory ball end up just where he wants it.

If he *did* have a brake on his wheel, this guy was good. He was thick-waisted and heavy across the chest and shoulders. Some solid muscle filled out that natty blue uniform coat. He had narrow eyes, a pencil mustache, and a mouth full of nice pearlies. Unlike the croupier who handled the bets, he smiled a lot. And if what I suspected was a fact, then he could afford to smile. He was crooking the customers out of some hefty lettuce.

If the wheel was braked, he was probably handling it with a foot control button under the table. I eased around behind him when he was busy smiling.

Bingo! There was a slight rise in the carpet under his right foot. *Very* slight. You'd really have to know what you were looking for to spot it, but I'd had a lot of practice. I kept watching him. Halfway through the next spin I saw the toe of his polished shoe press the rug lightly. There was no doubt about it, he was controlling the spin. And if this wheel was rigged, then they all were. Sylvia had been right. The action was dirty.

Which is when I felt another hand on my shoulder. It wasn't Scott Fitzgerald. This hand was hairy and thick-fingered and the body it belonged to would have delighted Japanese sports fans. This guy was built like a sumo wrestler. I mean, he was *big.*

"The boss wants you," he said. His fingers were digging into my shoulder and his pig eyes glittered; he was waiting for me to get tough. I intended to disappoint him. You don't argue with King Kong.

The boss was Tony Richetti.

When we got to his stateroom, which was plush as a sultan's palace, I got my first look at Richetti in the flesh. And there was a lot of it. I'd seen newspaper pictures of him, but I wasn't prepared for just how much he resembled Casper Gutman, my

17

oversized villain in *Falcon*. Not that Richetti was in the same class with the sumo wrestler who'd brought me here; no, he looked more like a fat pirate, in a pin-striped suit. He gave me a glare cold enough to freeze a penguin.

"I know who you are and I know what you're doing on the *Lady*," he said. His voice was like a rusty hinge.

I shrugged. "So?"

"You may be hot stuff back on shore," he said, "but out here you're dogshit."

"You run a crooked wheel, Richetti," I said levelly.

"I could kill you myself, right now, and nobody could prove anything," he said. "I pay enough money to the Coast Guard boys to keep them off my back. And the cops don't give a damn *what* happens out here."

He took a shiny black automatic out of his coat and put it on the desk.

"You plan to use that on me?" I said.

"I'm tempted, Hammett. Christ knows I'm tempted." And he caressed the gun like a pet cat.

"I'm internationally famous," I told him. "People around the world are reading my stuff. Shoot me and you'll be up to your fat ears in trouble. Even if you *do* grease the palms of some local lawboys." I grinned at him. "So you can put the gun away, Tony."

He did that, sliding it back into his coat. Then he gave me a pirate's smile. "You think I'm dumb enough to let you go—so you can spread the word my games are rigged?"

"What *are* you going to do with me?"

"I'm going to have my boys pour a quart of Scotch down your craw," he said, tenting his hands under his double chin. "Then I'll personally toss your ass into the Pacific." He chuckled, a Casper Gutman rumble. "And when your body is found, I'll tell the newspapers what a tragedy it is. Internationally famous au-

thor gets drunk on the *Lady* and falls overboard. A real tragedy."
I didn't respond to that.
There was nothing to say.

It would be nice to tell you I put up a hell of a fight and crippled two or three of Tony's boys with my flashing fists, but that's not the way it was.

The way it was, they poured a quart of Scotch down my craw, and Richetti personally tossed my ass into the Pacific.

The ocean was murderously cold, but I was so drunk by then I hardly felt it. Still, it didn't take long for me to realize I was in serious trouble.

First, I had to get rid of the booze. Alcohol causes the blood vessels to expand, making the body's heat loss a lot more severe. So I stuck my finger down my throat and vomited up a quart of good whiskey.

But even with most of the Scotch out of my stomach I knew that I couldn't last more than a half-hour. The numbing cold would finish me by then. My body reflexes would shut down, and I wouldn't be able to stay afloat.

Suddenly, a wave of dizziness hit me—and just before I blacked out I remember thinking about going down like the *Titanic*.

Then I quit thinking about anything.

THREE

I was looking at God.

He was grizzled and gray-bearded with a foghorn voice and sea-wrinkled eyes. A wide black rubber apron covered the swell of his gut and he wore hip-high rubber boots. The apron was splattered with blood and entrails; he'd been cleaning fish when he'd spotted me. His name was Hiram Withers and he had a son, Willy. It was their boat I was on.

"Tryin' to kill yourself, were you?" Withers asked. He was vigorously rubbing my arms and legs, restoring blood circulation. I was beginning to feel human again. "Lost your whole kit and kaboodle on the *Lady* and figured the ocean would solve all your problems." He grunted. "You're the first suicide we ever hauled in."

His son, a long-limbed youth with his father's glazed-blue sea eyes, nodded.

"I'm no suicide," I told them. "I was thrown overboard. Persona non grata on the *Lady*."

Withers raised a bushy eyebrow. "What the hell's *that*?"

"Skip it," I said. I felt weak and dizzy. "I'm just glad you two came along when you did."

"We sure enough took you for dead," muttered Willy, wrapping a dirty blanket around my shoulders. "You jus' weren't movin' none when we pulled you out of the drink."

"I owe you boys my life." Being alive made me emotional. "What can I do to repay you?"

Hiram Withers squinted at me. "Know anythin' about guttin' a fish?"

Happily, I was spared that onerous duty. When we docked later that morning I gave the pair of them the two hundred water-logged dollars I'd intended gambling with. (Richetti's boys hadn't bothered to lift my wallet.) I figured I'd won a bet with death and that Hiram and Willy deserved the payoff.

Ray Chandler and his wife lived like a couple of gypsies. Always on the move. From house to house, address to address. They moved somewhere new every four to six months.

They'd moved again since I'd seen Ray last (two months ago), but he'd phoned me his new address—a small wood frame one-story on a palm-shaded side street in Santa Monica. I knew I had the right place because Ray's big Duesy was parked in the red-brick driveway next to the house. His pride and joy—a cream-colored Duesenberg convertible, long and sleek and dignified, with the chrome polished to a glitter and the whitewalls well-scrubbed. Ray loved that machine the way a hunter loves his hound. It was the one stable thing in his unstable life. Beyond Cissy, of course. But, in my opinion, his love for Cissy bordered on the neurotic. Then again, Ray was neurotic about a lot of things.

Here he was, writing about private eyes, using a lot of tough underworld jargon that was as foreign to him as Greek to a goose. I'd lived on the mean streets; he just wrote about them. Product of a gentleman's education at Dulwich College in Merrie Olde England, he spoke with a British accent and had the habit of wearing white gloves to protect his hands when he typed.

He'd been born in Chicago but his mother had taken him to England when he was seven. He returned to the States in 1912, enlisted in the Canadian army in '17, and, two years later, was out of the service and living in Los Angeles. Went to work as a bookkeeper for Dabney Oil, married Cissy in 1924, and worked his way up to an executive level. By 1931 he was in charge of several smaller branch companies for the Dabney Syndicate. But booze got him fired in 1932 and he said to hell with office work. Decided to have a go at writing, selling his first story to Joe Shaw in 1933. And after that it was words, words, words. . . .

I left Buddy with the limo and walked up to Ray's front door, rang the buzzer. Eventually he answered, looking grumpy, like a bear who'd been routed from his winter cave. Had on a red silk bathrobe and his hair was tousled. He stood there inside the screen, blinking uneasily at me.

"Well, you sour son of a bitch, are you going to let me in?"

He unlatched the screen and swung it wide. "Sorry," he muttered, "but you should have called first."

"I *did* call," I told him. "Nobody answered."

He shrugged, tugging at the sash of his robe. "I don't fancy talking to people in the afternoon when I'm trying to write, so I don't answer the phone."

"It's morning, not afternoon," I pointed out.

"Same difference," Chandler muttered.

It's no use trying to argue with Ray; you always lose. He holds to his skewed brand of unwavering interior logic; he always knows what he means, even if you don't.

We passed through the front part of the house into his study. Actually, a second bedroom, lined with unpainted wooden bookcases. Chock-full of mysteries, biographies, and books on poison. Ray knows a lot about poison. There was a stack of manuscript pages on his desk and a page, half-typed, in his machine. Some framed photos of his early life in England were over the desk, along with one of him posing with his staff when he'd been an executive in the oil business.

He sat down at his desk and got a pipe going. I took the couch, flipping through an issue of *Black Mask*, the June '35 number.

"That's got my latest in it," Ray told me. "I had a swell title for it, but Shaw insisted on calling it 'Nevada Gas.' Sounds like a bowel problem."

"What was your title?"

"Doesn't matter." He exhaled a blue-gray plume of pipe smoke. "But it was swell."

"How much is Joe paying now?"

"Not enough," said Chandler. "Besides, why the deuce should you care? You're not writing for him anymore."

"Professional curiosity," I said. "Cissy home?"

Dumb question. Ray's wife was always home, safe inside their bedroom like a delicate hothouse flower that can't take direct sunlight. I could never figure why Ray married her—a woman eighteen years older than he was, bedridden most of the time with one odd malady or another. God knows he loved her. Worshiped is a better word. Told me he used to write poems to her and leave them on her pillow. Ray played it hard-nosed, but he was a confirmed romantic at heart.

"She's sleeping," he told me. He leaned forward, bending a silver paper clip in his fingers. "So, what's up, Dash? You look lousy."

"Hey, no matter how I look, I'm ahead of the game. I should be *dead*. Had a run-in with Tony Richetti on his ship last night. He threw me in the Pacific. Left me to drown. A fishing boat came along and pulled me out. I feel like Caesar's ghost."

Ray shook his head. "Don't tell me what happened between you and Richetti. I don't want to know. If I knew all the details

23

I might start to worry about you, and I can't afford to do that. I've got a new novelette to finish for Shaw."

"Fine," I said. "I didn't come here to discuss Tony Richetti."

"Then what *did* you come for?"

"To ask a big favor."

He put down his pipe, removed his glasses, and scrubbed at the bridge of his nose. "I don't have any money to give you. Don't you make enough at the studio? Christ, Dash, you make twenty times what I do. We're living off oil stock and there's not a lot of that left."

"I'm not asking for money," I told him. "I'm asking for some help, writer to writer."

"Help?"

"With the screen story I'm doing. *Blood Roads*. A gangster thing, a kind of Dillinger takeoff. It's right down your alley."

"I don't do screen work. That's your game."

"Hell, Ray, anybody who can write dialogue can write a script. It's dirt-simple once you get the hang of it. I know you can do it."

"The whole damn script?"

I grinned. "No, no. Only the last twenty pages. The rest is done."

"Why can't you finish it?"

I held up my right hand. "Sprained two fingers taking that dive overboard last night. Can't write. Can't type. And the final script is due on Monday."

"Jesus! This is Saturday!"

"So you do the twenty pages over the weekend." I tossed him a fat manila envelope I'd carried into the house. "It's all here— all but the end pages. C'mon, Ray, my ass is on the line. If I don't have this thing finished by Monday they won't renew my contract."

"Can't you dictate it?" asked Chandler. "Erle dictates everything he writes these days."

24

"I'm no Erle Stanley Gardner. I couldn't dictate my laundry list. I *need* this favor, Ray."

"All right, all right," he said, scowling at me. "But I'll have to go off the wagon again. I can't write a screenplay sober. Will you pay for the Scotch?"

"Absolutely," I said, smiling. "And I'll throw in two grand for the weekend's work."

He smiled. "Okay, you'll have the twenty pages by ten sharp Monday morning. That good enough?"

"Good enough," I said.

And I left to fetch the Scotch.

My sprained fingers got a lot better over the weekend. I found I could type again, which was a relief.

Entering the Global lot the following Monday afternoon, on my way to Bulow's office for a conference on *Blood Roads*, I ran into Heinie Faust, known in the writing game as "Max Brand," which is the most famous of his hatful of pen names. By descent, he's half-German and half-Irish. His real first name is Frederick, but he got tagged with the Teutonic nickname of "Heinie" when he was an undergrad at the University of California and it stuck. That's what his friends called him and I was one of them. Sort of. We weren't really friends in a technical sense.

We'd met in a New York bar two years ago when he was on a fiction assignment for *Collier's*. He lived in Italy most of the year, in a villa above the hills of Florence. Faust had read my *Glass Key* and liked it. Said he'd been influenced by it when he wrote one of his mysteries, *The Night Flower*. Mainly he wrote Westerns, tons of them. Told me he'd turned out thirteen million words just for one pulp magazine alone—Street & Smith's *Western Story*. That kind of massive word production addled my mind, but Heinie didn't seem to think anything of it. Prose didn't mean much to him: only classical verse counted. Heinie was a frustrated poet.

We'd talked the night away back in New York in a conversation that ran the gamut from the eloquence of Greek poetry to the value of a good right cross in boxing. From breeding bull terriers to riding thoroughbreds in Kentucky. From Napoleon's campaign at Austerlitz to the flaws in Shakespeare's *Tempest*. He was one hell of a talker, was Heinie. When the sun came up he was gone, and I hadn't seen or heard from him since.

Now he was wearing the same wrinkled gray suit I'd seen him in two years ago, or one just like it. He was a big fellow, over six three, with wide shoulders and a chiseled face that had seen some hard living. His hands were chunky, sun-freckled, square-fingered. I asked him what he was doing at Global.

"They brought me out to develop a new Western for Mix," he told me. "But I just talked to Bulow, and said to hell with it."

I was surprised to hear this. When Tom Mix made his jump from silents to talkies he'd done it with one of Faust's novels, *Destry Rides Again*. I'd read about it in the trades. Heinie and Mix seemed an ideal match.

"What went wrong?"

"Everything," Faust growled. "Mix can't handle spoken dialogue. Did you see that serial he just finished for Mascot, *The Miracle Rider*? Jesus Christ on a mountain but it was godawful!"

"I don't see many Westerns."

"Well, Mix is a disaster. Stolid. Flat-voiced. Wooden. And he's too damn old to do his own stunt riding, so most of it had to be doubled. I told Bulow I was off the project. I'm heading back to Italy. Hollywood is too phony for me."

"Leaving when?"

"Right away," he said. Then he gave me a lopsided grin. "Sorry we can't tie one on at Musso's. If I'd known you were on the lot I'd have looked you up."

"Same here," I said.

We shook hands. His grip was firm.

"You going to be coming back in the near future?" I asked.

"Not if I can help it. To me, Southern California's like one big stage set. If it ever got hit by a Texas twister there wouldn't be a damn thing left. It'd just all vanish in the wind. Europe is substantial. Has roots. Everything's sand out here, and roots don't stick in sand."

"I'm not all that crazy about it myself," I admitted. "But the money's good."

"I'll stay with magazine writing. I've done okay with that."

He clapped me on the shoulder. "Watch out for twisters, Dash!" Then he gave me another lopsided grin. "Adios."

I watched him walk away in his long-legged, fast-moving stride. Max Brand, the King of the Pulps. Classic thinker. Frustrated poet. Would he ever be lured back to Angeltown?

I doubted it.

Ernie Bulow had a face like an inverted pyramid: wide, bald head, narrow slate-colored eyes that told you he didn't trust anybody, thin cheeks, and a chin sharp enough to open letters with. Bulow's family owned a string of warehouses back in Chicago and he got into the movie game when his Uncle Charlie decided it would be dandy to run a film studio. He tried to buy out RKO but they wouldn't sell. So Charlie founded Global, promptly dropped dead of a stroke, and left the studio to his favorite nephew. Suddenly, at forty-five, Ernie found himself in Hollywood, chasing starlets around his authentic Louis Quatorze desk, and smoking two-dollar Cuban cigars. He had one in the corner of his mouth when I walked into his office late Monday afternoon. (I'd had the completed script—including Ray's last twenty pages—delivered to him at ten that morning.)

"I've read your screenplay, Samuel," he told me. (My full name is Samuel Dashiell Hammett, but everybody in Hollywood calls me Dash. Everybody but Ernie.)

"And?"

"And it's a breather."

I was confused. Did he like it or didn't he? Feeling stupid, I repeated the word: "Breather?"

He walked over to grip my right arm at the elbow, giving it a squeeze. "It lives! It breathes! It holds the essence of life!" He was punctuating the air with puffs of dense cigar smoke. "Especially the last twenty pages. Genius, Samuel, pure genius! You write like a slumming angel."

"Thanks," I said. I decided not to tell Ray about the "genius" part; he'd probably ask for another grand.

Bulow tapped a finger against the script on his desk. "Swear to God I had tears in my eyes at the end," he said. "That dialogue where she tells him goodbye as he's about to croak in the gutter . . ." He looked at me intently. "I gotta tellya, if he were still around, Shakespeare would be jealous."

"Well . . ." I shrugged. "I'm . . . uh . . . glad you like it."

"We'll shoot the whole thing exactly as written," he assured me.

"Then I guess there's no problem about renewing my contract."

"Consider it done, including your raise," Ernie said, easing back against the edge of his leather-topped desk, his eyes locked on mine. "Now all you have to do is tell us where she is."

"Where *who* is?"

"Sylvia, of course," he said softly. Ernie walked over to the wall, staring up at a large, bronze-framed publicity portrait of Sylvia Vane. She had her long-lashed eyes lowered to half-mast and the slinky jade silk evening gown she wore was more off than on, showing what she had. Which was plenty. "I refer to our beloved star," Ernie continued, his eyes still on the picture. "Your current paramour."

"Afraid you're a bit ahead of yourself in that department," I told him. "Sad to say, nothing of an erotic nature has transpired between us. Not *yet* anyway. But I'm curious. How'd you happen to make the connection?"

"Sylvia's a tongue-wagger," Bulow said, turning to face me. "She told a friend of hers that she was going to owe you some sexual favors. I just assumed there had been a payoff."

"Well, there *hasn't*," I said. "And besides, Ernie, realistically speaking, it's none of your damn business what goes on between me and Sylvia Vane."

"There you are wrong, Samuel," he said, lighting a fresh cigar. "Everything she does is my business. I'm paying her an arm and a leg to star in *Blood Roads*. She was due in for a wardrobe test today, but she never showed."

"Did you call her house?"

"Three times. No answer. I even sent a boy over, but she didn't come to the door. Frankly, I don't think she's there. But I'll wager you know where she is."

"Flat on her back and sexually exhausted after our weekend orgy, right?"

"Something like that."

"Why don't you go suck a duck?"

His face reddened. "You're off the picture, Hammett, and you can forget about a contract renewal—"

I grinned at him. A tight, wicked grin. "You know what you can do with that, don't you, Ernie?"

I pulled the cigar from his mouth, snapped it in half, and walked out into the bright sunshine.

I was steamed. I don't mind working for these studio bosses with their elephant-sized egos and pea-sized brains, but when they start telling me how to run my love life I cut the string.

This situation was really one big tickle. I'd just lost my job over an affair I'd never started. I was strictly virgin where Sylvia Vane was concerned. In fact, I'd had no word from her since

Friday when we'd had our little talk about Richetti. I'd tried to phone her with what I'd discovered about his roulette wheels, but she hadn't picked up.

Maybe Ernie was wrong; maybe she *was* in her mansion after all. Could be she'd tied one on over the weekend and was nursing a colossal hangover.

I decided to find out.

FOUR

Buddy took me over to Sylvia's place, parking the limo in the wide circular drive which directly fronted her house—an unfortunate blend of Southern Colonial and Italian Renaissance, with red Spanish tiles on the roof. There were marble statues on the lawn and tall white pillars on the wide veranda. I pressed the door buzzer and heard chimes ring inside the house. No response. More chimes, same result.

I told Buddy to sit tight and walked around to the service porch. Got out my pocket knife and pried open the door. Right away, even here in the kitchen area, I smelled the sharp scent of iron. Decaying blood, unmistakable. There were other smells, too, and I liked them even less. It didn't take me long to find Sylvia, sprawled in the hallway. She was in a skimpy black-lace negligee, lying face down. She'd been stabbed. It had taken a while for her to die and her heart had pumped out a lot of blood on the porous Spanish floor tiles. Somebody was going to have a hell of a clean-up job.

I left her there, went to the kitchen phone and called Beverly Hills Homicide. "Sylvia Vane is dead," I told the cop who answered. "A knife job." I didn't have to give the address;

31

Beverly Hills cops always know where the hometown celebrities live.

"Who is this?" he demanded. "Who's calling?"

"J. Edgar Hoover," I said, hanging up.

I wiped my prints off the phone and the back door and got the hell out.

On the way home I told Buddy what I'd found. It ended there. He would never let the cops know we'd been over to Sylvia's, even if they asked. Like most Haitians, he had a mouth like a locked safe. Voodoo is the religion down there and people learn early to keep their traps shut. Oh, Haitians can be plenty affable—Buddy, like most of his fellow islanders, was always great company—but secrets having to do with the dead are not to be trifled with. Not when you believe, as Buddy did, that the dead can be reanimated.

I fixed myself a double-dip strawberry soda in the rumpus room to get my thoughts off Sylvia. But I couldn't. Her dead image filled my mind—that lovely white skin stained by dried blood. Even her beautiful blonde hair had been soaked in it.

Richetti. Yeah, Tony Richetti had to be the boy. Sylvia couldn't pay him the fifty gees she owed him so he closed the account. I could tip the law to Richetti, but nothing would happen. He owned City Hall. He could walk in there and ice the mayor and they wouldn't lay a glove on him.

The Vane murder was big news. SEX SIREN STABBED . . . VIO-LENT DEATH IN BEVERLY HILLS . . . STAR FALLS VICTIM TO MURDER. The press had a field day, running shots of sultry Sylvia in a variety of sex-drenched studio poses.

On page two of the *Examiner* there were tearful quotes about the dead star from a host of illustrious Hollywood personalities from Gable to Cecil B. DeMille. Heading the list, an accolade from Ernie Bulow himself, who called her "a glorious goddess of light, now forever dimmed." I nearly gagged on that one.

Naturally, nobody fingered Richetti for the knife job. On the radio, Walter Winchell complained about "the staggering amount of everyday violence troubling our great nation" and how poor Sylvia Vane was most probably the victim of an armed intruder whom she was unfortunate enough to encounter in the act of robbing her home. Sure. And the moon's made of green cheese.

I'd just snapped off the radio, catching Winchell in mid-staccato, when the phone rang. It was Joe Shaw, calling from his office at *Black Mask* in the heart of New York to tell me how shocked he was over Sylvia's murder. He sounded really shaken and I couldn't figure it. Why all the heavy emotion over a dead movie star he'd never met?

"You're wrong about that," Joe said in that gravel voice of his. "At one time, Sylvia meant the world to me. She was the most wildly passionate woman I've ever known."

That rocked me. "You had an affair with Sylvia Vane?"

"Her name was Vanikis when I knew her," he said. "She changed it when she went to Hollywood."

"Well, I feel for you, Joe. If there's anything I can do. . . ."

"You can take the next train here, that's what you can do. I've got to see you right away, Dash. My daughter's life depends on it."

That one rocked me again. "Daughter? I never knew you *had* a daughter. Are you telling me that you and Sylvia—"

"Yes. Clare was born in 1914, when Sylvia was nineteen."

"You're certainly full of surprises."

"I'll give you all the details when you get here. But time's running out. I need your help to save Clare's life. Will you come?"

"You know I'll come," I told him. "But there's something else behind this, isn't there?"

"The Cat's Eye," said Joe softly. "It's all about the Cat's Eye."

On the train east I had plenty of time to think about Joe Shaw and the Cat's Eye. . . .

When Joseph Thompson Shaw was hired to take over *Black Mask* in 1926 he didn't know beans about editing a pulp. Oh, sure, he'd edited his campus paper at Bowdoin College in Maine, and he'd written some scattered stuff before the War, but Joe was basically a soldier of fortune. Loved boats and sailing and athletics. Became a master of the sword, winning a national championship in sabers. During the Great War in Europe he was a bayonet instructor and made Captain—which was why a lot of his writers still call him "Cap." He'd gone on to head relief missions in Czechoslovakia and Greece for several years. When the publishers of *Black Mask* hired him, Shaw admitted he'd never read a single issue of their magazine. But Joe is sharp, tough, and hard-working—and he really took hold of *Mask*, improved its format, got some top names to write for it, and shot up its circulation. He even lured me back into the fold. I'd quit *Mask* by the time Joe came along, but he pep-talked me into extending a couple of my Continental Op stories to novel length. That got me back into *Mask* and started my book career. Without Joe, it might never have happened. He's a great editor and an easy guy to like.

After the two Op novels, I told told Joe I wanted to switch to a new protagonist. I had an idea for doing a story about a San Francisco private detective with dubious morals who played both sides of the law and always came out on top. But I needed a gizmo. Something that would fully involve my shady hero and the crooks he tangled with. Something they all wanted and would kill to get.

That's when Joe told me about this family heirloom he kept in his office safe. A human skull inlaid with precious stones, including a fat red ruby gleaming in one of its eye sockets. He claimed it had a lethal history going all the way back to Richard the Lion-Heart.

According to Joe, it started in the 1100s with King Richard and the Crusades. Richard was out to get the Holy Land back from the infidels, but he wasn't above grabbing some choice loot in the bargain. When he recaptured the port of Jaffa from Saladin, the great Muslim warrior, in 1192, part of the booty he liberated was this jeweled skull with the big shining ruby in it. He named it the Cat's Eye. But on Richard's way back to England he was captured in Austria by Duke Leopold who stuck him in a dungeon and took away all his stolen treasure, including the skull.

A full century later the Cat's Eye popped up in Tangiers, where more blood was spilled over it. The skull surfaced again in Italy, where a lusty prince gave it to his lady love. Then a Turkish rug dealer latched onto the gizmo and sold it to a fat-bucks businessman in Constantinople. But not long after that a Russian general snuffed the rich guy for it.

So that's how things went, with the Cat's Eye being nabbed over and over again down the centuries, including the time it was stolen by an enterprising member of the French Expedition to Mongolia. Joe was never quite sure just how his ancestors managed to end up with it, but he told me it had been in the family for generations.

When he finished his story I knew he'd just handed me a winner. Bang, I had *The Maltese Falcon*. I transferred the jeweled skull into a jeweled falcon and made up my own blood history. Then all I had to do was create some characters desperate enough to kill each other for it, and stick my detective in the middle of the action. Private detectives do a lot of spade work, digging for clues, so that seemed like an appropriate last name for him. When I was a Pink, everyone called me Sam, so I added it to the mix. Result: Sam Spade.

Joe ran the novel as a five-part serial in *Mask*, raving over it in his editorials. It got picked up for hardcover by Knopf, earned some excellent reviews (one of them rating me with Hemingway), and was snapped up by Warner Brothers. The film rights became my ticket to Hollywood where the greenbacks began to flood in. A lot less work for a lot more money, a combination I appreciated.

I thought about all this on the train as it rattled across country. Obviously, Joe Shaw and the Cat's Eye were very much back in my life.

Joe met me at Grand Central Station. The fall weather had a bite to it and he was wearing a long tweed coat over his pinstripe. He'd put on some weight since I'd seen him last and a thick brush mustache sprouted under his nose. He told me I looked "half starved" and that I needed to eat more.

"I eat fine," I said. "I've been skinny all my life. I was skinny when I wrote for you, remember?"

"Sure, but you had TB in those days. You're over it now, right?"

I'd first been diagnosed as having tuberculosis in 1919 when I was still in the army. I'd been down with Spanish influenza a year earlier, when it was running rampant in all the army camps, and the flu had damaged my lungs, leaving me wide open to TB. Because of it, I got a medical discharge, and when I felt a little stronger I went back to work for Pinkerton's. By 1920 I was in the hospital again, getting out in the spring of '21. I worked for awhile, quit Pinkerton's in '22, got hit with a TB flare-up in '24, and had it off and on into 1929 when the docs pronounced me cured.

Now I told Joe: "Sure, I'm over the TB—but I'm still the original thin man. Nothing's going to change that. Now can we switch subjects? I didn't take a train all the way here from L.A. to discuss my weight."

"We'll talk at the office," Joe said.

Outside the station, we took a taxi over to the *Black Mask* building at 25 West Forty-fifth. New York was New York. And despite the breadlines, even in these grim Depression days, it was still Bigtown, U.S.A. The city that never sleeps. Full of people in a hurry to go somewhere or get back from going somewhere. Blaring auto horns. Sidewalk preachers shouting Armageddon. Street vendors selling hot dogs and pickles. Fancy ladies selling themselves. I felt the pulse of raw street life around me and I liked the feeling.

I'd written *The Thin Man* here two years ago at the Sutton Club Hotel on East 56th when Lily had been with me. We'd had some fine times together in this town. She kept nagging me about getting back into the detective business and drove me half-batty asking endless questions about my years with Pinkerton. So I wrote her into the book as Nora Charles who rags Nick into taking on another case. Lily told me she didn't recognize herself as Nora. That was just before she became Miss Lillian Hellman, Great American Playwright. I hadn't seen much of her lately, but we've got something special going for us. And I guess we always will.

Joe's office was like all editorial offices. Jammed with work folders, manuscripts, artwork, and page spreads for the next issue, with phones ringing and staffers running around wearing harried faces. Framed *Black Mask* covers under glass lined all four walls, portraying gangsters in slouch hats with blazing tommy guns, damsels in required distress, uniformed motor cops with smoking revolvers—all in gaudy primary colors. Several of the covers had my name splashed across them. They reminded me of the sweating night hours in Frisco in the '20s when I'd poured out all those words on my faithful Smith Corona, when each *Black Mask* check paid another overdue bill. I *had* to be prolific back then or I didn't eat.

Joe pushed a stack of art samples off the leather couch and told me to sit. He had a lot to say.

Shutting his office door, he instructed his mousy-looking secretary to hold his calls, then took the chair next to me. His eyes looked haunted, and his skin was flushed; he was ready to tell me some painful things.

"You need to know the full truth," he said. "About me and Sylvia. And about Clare. Even my closest friends have never heard what I'm going to tell you."

"Do they know you have a daughter?"

He shook his head. "I've walled off that part of my life."

"Go on," I said.

"It began twenty-two years ago, right here in New York," said Joe. "I'd returned from a research trip to Europe. I was a travel writer in those days."

"Yeah," I said. "You showed me that book you did on Spain. Something about the Dons."

"*A Narrative Guide to the Country of the Dons*," said Shaw. "And it didn't sell worth bird crap. Guess I wasn't meant to write travel books."

"So—how did you meet Sylvia?"

"She'd just turned eighteen. Her head was full of dreams about becoming a fashion model. To make ends meet, she was working as a maid in the hotel where I was staying. One look at her when she walked into my room to make the bed and I was a goner."

I nodded. "She was a peach, all right."

"She told me she had ambitions, that she really wanted to

become a model. I knew some people, made some calls, and got her an interview with a small agency here in town. And she clicked. Sylvia had just the look they wanted. She was able to quit her maid's job to model full-time."

"How did you get into an affair with her?"

Joe scrubbed at his mustache. "It happened fast. As I told you, she was very passionate. A real wildcat in bed. We lived together for just over a year, until she had Clare. I'd given her an emerald engagement ring that had originally belonged to my grand-mother, but Sylvia didn't see herself playing the role of wife and mother. I begged her to marry me, but she said no, that she had a career to pursue. In films. By that time she was desperate to be a movie star."

He opened a desk drawer, took out a photo, handed it to me. "This was taken a month after Clare was born. The ring on Sylvia's hand is the one I gave her."

The photo showed a teenaged Sylvia squinting into the sun, holding a dark-haired baby girl in her arms. The emerald ring was clearly visible.

"Clare had the most beautiful big brown eyes," Joe told me proudly.

"So Sylvia took off for Hollywood?" I asked.

"No, first she went to Canada for a few years. Toronto. She took acting classes there, got enough work to support herself and Clare, began to make a name for herself. Then, when Clare was six, they came back. Sylvia made arrangements to send Clare to a childless family in West Virginia. That's where Clare was raised, by this family."

"And you just let it happen? Hell, Joe, she was *your* daughter, too!"

"I know, I know." He shook his head. "But Sylvia and I weren't married, and I was broke back then. I just couldn't take care of a kid. Clare needed a family."

"What happened to your grandmother's emerald ring? Did Sylvia give it back to you?"

"No. She added a gold chain and put it around Clare's neck. I assume Clare still has it."

"Did you stay in touch with your daughter?"

He shook his head. "How could I? Sylvia refused to tell me what family had taken Clare or what town they lived in. Some years later Clare found out that I was her blood father and she phoned me. She was still living in West Virginia then, but she wouldn't tell me where."

"Was she in touch with Sylvia?"

"I don't think so. Of course, by then she knew Sylvia was her birth mother, but Clare wouldn't talk about her. Her birthday was coming up, her eighteenth. That was the same age Sylvia had been when I met her. By that time I had some money. I mailed a silver necklace from Cartier's to a post office box number Clare had given me. After she got it, she phoned again to thank me for it. That was three years ago and I haven't heard from her, or *about* her, until now—until I got this."

He handed me a letter typed on anonymous five-and-dime stationery:

Shaw—

Sylvia's death is a warning. To prove to you that I'm serious. I know about the Cat's Eye and I propose a simple trade. The skull for your daughter's life. Leave it in locker S27 at the Santa Fe train station in Pasadena. Have your pal Hammett bring the skull to California and put it in the locker before midnight on the 31st of this month. Tell him to tape the key to the back of the locker facing the wall. I've got Clare, and unless I get the Cat's Eye, she'll die like her mother. If you don't believe me, I've enclosed the proof.

There was no signature, but there were some handwritten words at the bottom of the page.

No tricks. If there's a stakeout on the locker I'll spot it and you won't ever see your daughter alive again.

"Where's the proof?" I asked Joe.

He dropped a silver necklace into my hand. "This is what I sent Clare for her eighteenth birthday."

"Are you sure it's genuine?"

"Her name is on the inside of the locket. See for yourself."

He was right. The fine engraving said: *To Clare, with love.*

"Okay," I said. "Suppose I deliver the skull. Put it in the locker. The killer gets it and goes ahead and knifes Clare anyway, to shut her up. Murderers and kidnappers are not known for keeping their word."

"What else can I do?" asked Joe. There was agony in his face. "If I don't turn over the skull I'm *certain* she'll be killed. And I can't take that chance. I have to believe that once the skull is delivered Clare will be freed."

"Before I came here I thought I knew who killed Sylvia," I told Joe. "This note confirms it."

"The note's unsigned. How do you know who sent it?"

"Believe me, Tony Richetti sent it."

"The gambling king?"

"Yeah. He owns *The Wicked Lady.* Sylvia went there a lot. Played the wheels. She was into Richetti for fifty big ones. My hunch is, he found out about the Cat's Eye—how I don't know—and put this little murder-kidnap act together."

"The Cat's Eye is worth a great deal more than fifty thousand," declared Shaw. "Actually, closer to a million."

"Obviously, Tony decided to collect some interest."

"How can you be so certain that the note's from him?"

41

"Handwriting at the bottom. Sylvia showed me a letter he sent her, telling her to pay up or else. Same hand. Sprawling O's, low-crossed T-bars dipping down. It's from friend Tony all right."

"I can't understand how he found out about Sylvia's having a daughter—or that I was Clare's father."

"Maybe Sylvia told him," I said. "At least we know he's behind all this."

"How did he find Clare?"

I shrugged.

Joe gave me a sharp look. "At this point, with my daughter's life in the balance, I don't want you going to the police."

"Wouldn't dream of it," I said. "Tony's too cozy with the law in L.A. Plays golf with the mayor. Got a lot of heft in City Hall."

"Then do exactly as he says in the letter." Shaw turned to a large framed oil portrait of President Roosevelt hanging on the wall above his desk. I knew that Joe practically worshiped FDR. He was a rabid New Deal man and enthusiastically supported Roosevelt's WPA work program, which had recently been put into effect. Now Joe took down the painting, revealing a safe in the wall behind it.

"I keep the skull here," he said, spinning the combination dial. The safe swung open and Joe removed a football-sized package. "This is it."

I'd never seen Joe's treasure. I stripped away the thick brown wrapping paper, feeling like Sam Spade uncovering the falcon for the first time. Life imitating fiction. Finally, there it was, gleaming in my hand. The Cat's Eye. A large, perfect ruby winked at me from the skull's left eye socket.

"Jeez!" I said under my breath. "The thing's covered with stones."

"All prime quality," said Joe. "Diamonds, rubies, emeralds, pearls. . . ."

"Richetti can never sell this baby on the open market," I told Shaw, slowly turning the jeweled skull in my hands. "But there are private collectors who'd pay through the nose for it." I wrapped the skull again. "Got something to carry it in?"

Joe brought out a square leather case. His look was intense. "Until you get it to Pasadena, don't let it out of your sight. Not for a second."

"Gotcha," I said. "I'll even take it into the crapper with me."

We shook hands. There wasn't a lot left to say. It galled me, playing delivery boy for Richetti, but I'd do it for Joe's sake.

And to save a life.

FIVE

The train ride back to California gave me more time to ponder. I sat by the window, watching the towns and houses and cars flicker past like postcard images, and I did a lot of pondering. I pondered the question of just why Richetti had named me as the courier.

Naturally, he knew about my having written for *Mask*, and that Joe and I were pals. Public knowledge. Maybe he planned to finish the job he'd started when he had me pitched into the drink. The papers had picked up the story of my ocean rescue, so he knew I was still alive. He knew I'd tell Sylvia about his crooked wheel and figured it was a good time to get rid of her. She'd threatened to warn all of her gambling friends about him.

But then along comes this bid for the Cat's Eye and his note saying *that's* why he iced Sylvia, to shake up Joe Shaw. Well, maybe he got rid of her for both reasons—because she'd threatened him and because he wanted to make Joe fork over the skull.

That brought me full-circle back to my original question: why did Richetti tag *me* for the delivery? Sure, he knew Joe would trust me with the Cat's Eye, but why not have Shaw deliver it personally? Unless Tony planned to get rid of me once the skull was inside the locker. It was a perfect set-up if that was his plan; he'd know exactly when and where to strike.

It was late in the evening when the train arrived in Pasadena. Carrying the leather case, I walked directly toward the rows of metal lockers adjacent to the depot's main waiting room. The area was swarming like a hive—with people taking trains or getting off trains. I ran my eyes over the crowd. Any one of them could be working for Tony, waiting to make sure I finished my delivery job before finishing me.

Ease up, Hammett, you're getting paranoid. If I'd been this jumpy in the Pinkerton days I wouldn't have stayed an op for long. I'd learned to play it loose and easy back then—but I wasn't a detective now, I was a writer. And writers sweat more.

I found S27 without any fuss, the end locker on the inside second row. Got it open. Looked around. Everything seemed okay. I was just hefting the square leather case onto the green metal locker shelf when somebody sapped me—and the world exploded into a million swirling black fragments.

I woke up in Hell.

A ring of grotesque figures surrounded me, peering down, their faces fanged and horrible: a demon, a witch, a crimson devil, and a hunchback dwarf with taloned fingers.

Then I remembered what night it was. October thirty-first. Halloween. These were costumed children, curious about the grown man who had fallen on the floor between a row of lockers.

"Are you dead, mister?" the witch asked me. Her voice was tiny and piping.

"I don't think so," I told her. My head was ringing like a bell and it was tough getting things into focus.

"Shoo! You kids move back, now!"

A big depot cop was leaning over me, brass buttons glittering. "You okay, fella?"

"I'm just swell," I said, sitting up.

"Took yourself quite a tumble," the beefy cop said. "What happened?"

"Blacked out," I told him. "I've got a condition."

"Condition?"

"Belgian swamp fever. From the Congo."

The cop nodded. "I heard of that, all right. Aunt of mine had the same thing."

"Sorry to cause all the commotion."

The beefcake helped me to stand as the people around me murmured about jungle fever.

"You gotta watch yourself," the cop said. "Sure you're all right now?"

"Right as rain," I said. I glanced at the open locker shelf.

It was empty.

I took a cab from the train station in Pasadena to Hollywood. To Erle Stanley Gardner's house. I'd worked on a film job with Erle at Paramount a few months earlier, before I took on the *Blood Roads* project for Global. Our script was based on one of his Speed Dash, Human Fly pulp stories, *Three Days to Midnight*. It was all pretty silly stuff and the script was never produced, but the two of us get along famously. (Except for his nagging me about my smoking.) Right now Erle was hot in the industry due to the way his new Perry Mason character had taken off. Seven Mason books had been published over the past couple of years. Warner Brothers had a contract on Mason and they were already cranking out a string of films with Warren William as Erle's fighting lawyer.

Gardner was an incredibly fast wordsmith, right up there with Max Brand in terms of productivity. In fact, he told me he'd sold something like four hundred short stories and novelettes *before* he wrote his first novel!

He had started as a lawyer in Oxnard, in California's Ventura County, and established a reputation as a fighter for the underdog against superior legal odds. Obviously, he was his own model for Perry Mason—both of them stubborn, tough, and quick-thinking. Difference is, Erle didn't win every case he took to court.

As a writer, Gardner broke into print in the early 1920s and quickly began selling to a wide variety of pulps. He'd carry on his busy law practice by day, bone up on past cases at the law library in the evenings, then pound out several thousand words of fiction each night, surviving on just three hours of sleep. Finally he decided that his typewriter wasn't fast enough. To speed up his wordage, he switched to a Dictaphone, letting his secretary do the typing. Told me that he'd dictated the first Mason novel, *The Case of the Velvet Claws*, in just four days.

When the first two Masons were published in 1933, Erle was still a working lawyer, but that part of his life was winding down. After the books took off and Hollywood got interested, he hung up his shingle to write full-time. Ended up buying a house in the Hollywood hills, but he doesn't like to be pinned down in one place. City life bores him: Erle is a natural outdoorsman who loves camping. Especially in the desert. Told me that being out there in all that open space gives him "a pure feeling." Once the movie money began coming his way he had a rolling campertrailer custom built to his specifications and he keeps it parked in the yard behind his house between trips.

That's where I found him.

His Filipino houseboy told me that "Mister Erle" was working in the camper. There was no outside light, so he led me down a very dark side path, around a spreading flower garden, to a large open concrete patio. Erle's big trailer was parked there, looking like a silver blimp in the moonlight.

I banged on the metal door and he yelled for me to come in.

Inside, Erle was sprawled on a bamboo couch in work pants and a white pullover sweater, a Dictaphone mike in his hand. Slipping a fresh cylinder into the machine, he waved me to a lawn chair. (I had to remove a length of rubber hose to clear it.) The camper was jammed with sports gear and the paraphernalia of outdoor life: a collapsible tent, an archery target (Erle was like Robin Hood when it came to a bow), tennis racquets, several canteens, fishing poles and bait buckets, a portable cookstove, blankets and rain gear, shelved cans of food, skis, lawn furniture, a hand-tooled leather bag of golf clubs—even a bicycle pegged to one of the curving walls.

Erle was dictating the wrap-up to a Jenkins Phantom Crook story. Full of violence and flashing guns—in direct contrast to his more cerebral Mason courtroom sagas. He'd been selling to *Black Mask* since 1923, and his Ed Jenkins novelettes were very popular with *Mask* readers. They kept demanding more, and Erle happily filled the demand, doing several each year to keep Joe Shaw happy. Now, pushing his glasses to the edge of his nose, he gave me a smile, put aside the microphone, and clicked off the machine.

"Happy Halloween, Dash," he said, his round, cheerful face radiating good will. "I just heard about the murder of your leading lady. *You* didn't kill her, did you?"

"I never kill beautiful women. You should know that by now."

"How's all this going to affect your picture?"

"It's not my picture anymore," I told him. "Had my butt kicked off the project after I insulted the head of the studio."

"Sorry to hear that."

"Don't be. The guy's a real piece of worm shit. I enjoyed telling him off."

"Typical of your cavalier attitude toward the working dollar. You want me to recommend you as writer on the next Mason script for Warner's, is that it?"

"No, that isn't it," I said. "God, Erle, how you love jumping to conclusions."

"A habit of mine," he admitted. "I end up treating people like characters in my fiction."

He leaned back, scowling. "And speaking of my characters, have you *seen* any of the Mason pictures?"

"No. Have I missed anything?"

"Hell, no, you haven't! Warner's done three of 'em so far and each one's worse than the last. When they couldn't get Bill Powell for *The Case of the Howling Dog* they signed Warren William. He is distinctly *not* Mason. In *Howling Dog* they had him as head of a huge law firm if you can believe it, with squads of partners and secretaries. Then, in *Curious Bride*, they moved him to San Francisco and had him whipping up crab dishes as a gourmet cook, for Christ's sake! How I hate that damn picture!"

"They made a third one, right?"

"Sure, they royally screwed up *Lucky Legs*. Mason's practically an alcoholic! In the picture he's got a whole closet filled with liquor. And that's all your fault!"

I blinked at that one. "My fault?"

"Once your *Thin Man* hit big, Warner's insisted on turning Mason into Nick Charles, a wisecracking drunk."

"I have nothing to do with what those studio chowderheads dream up, and you know it."

He sighed. "You're right. I'm just letting off steam. Mason's the best thing I have going for me right now and I tend to get over-protective about him. It's tough, watching them rape my character at Warner's."

"Don't let it throw you," I told him. "Books are one thing and films are another. The movies have an entirely different audience. No studio can hurt your books. They'll go right on selling to mystery readers—like a snowball rolling downhill. And it's *your* snowball."

"I guess so. . . ." Erle shook his head. "The truth is, I wish you *would* write the next Mason script. You'd put things right." He smiled suddenly, pointing at me. "Hey, you've quit smoking!"

"How do you know that?"

"You'd have one of the damn things in your mouth by now."

"Okay, so I'm trying to stay off cigarettes," I admitted. "For the moment, it seems to be working. I chew up a lot of pencils."

"I'm proud of you," Erle declared. He adjusted his glasses. "So if you don't want to horn in on the Mason money factory, why *are* you here?"

"What if I said I was paying a social call, just to see how a pal is doing?"

"I wouldn't believe you." His eyes gleamed. "You've got some kind of caper in mind and you think I can help."

He'd nailed me. "I do—and you can."

"And I'll bet it has something to do with Sylvia Vane's murder."

"Right again, Mr. Mason." I picked up a wooden tent peg, began twisting it in my hands. "Your fishing boat. I need to borrow it."

Gardner gave me a sly grin and his eyes twinkled. When he did that he reminded me of Santa Claus. Not that he was anywhere near that heavy, but he *was* on the chunky side, with those twinkling eyes set into his round-cheeked face. Avuncular. That's the word. Which is why women usually called him "Uncle Erle."

"My boat is like my camper," he said. "I don't lend either of them to anybody. Rules of the house."

"This is really serious, Erle. There's a girl's life in the balance."

He scowled. "Then quit fiddling with that damn tent peg and tell me about it."

I did. All of it, the whole story, including the details of Shaw's affair with Sylvia and about their daughter, and how Clare's kidnapping was tied into the Cat's Eye. Even gave him a capsule history of the skull, and how I was sure that Richetti had it and was continuing to hold Shaw's daughter captive aboard the *Lady*. "I don't trust Tony to keep his promise about turning her loose. He's not that dumb."

"Why didn't he kill you when he had the chance at the train station in Pasadena?" Erle asked me. "Why just sap you down? He could have put a blade in your ribs."

"Maybe he knows I'll come for Clare and wants the fun of killing me aboard the *Lady*."

"You intend going out there after her?"

"That's the reason I need to borrow your boat. I still haven't learned how to walk on water."

"This is suicide," he told me. "Besides, knowing Richetti, Clare's probably dead by now."

"Probably."

"And even if she's alive when you get out there, he'll just go ahead and kill you both."

"Probably," I said again.

"What makes you think you can pull off a rescue?"

"I'll go out in the early morning, when the fog is thickest. I'll anchor just beyond the *Lady* and swim over to her, then make sure no one sees me climb aboard."

"Even if you manage all that, how will you find Clare?"

"I've been to Richetti's private cabin area, so I know the layout. If I find her alive I'll do a fast fade back to your boat and call in the Coast Guard. Even Tony Richetti can't buy his way out of a kidnapping."

"Will you be carrying?"

"Yeah, a .38 Police Positive with a four-inch barrel—in a waterproof holster. And I'll use it if I have to."

"Sounds real Wild West," Erle said. "Also real stupid. You'll never make it off the *Lady.*"

"That's my concern," I said tightly.

"No, it's our concern. You'll be using *my* damn boat!"

I leaned forward. "Then you'll let me have it?"

"Providing I'm along to see that nothing happens to my pride and joy. After they rub you out I'll be there to run it safely back to shore. That's my deal. If you're set on this insanity, then *I* go along with my boat."

"Aye, aye, Cap'n."

"When do we leave?" Erle asked.

"Late tonight. If we cast off an hour before sunup that ought to be about right. We can time it to reach the *Lady* a tad before dawn. They'll have to shut down the action and most of the crew should be sleeping. We'll use the fog as a cover."

"Okay," said Gardner, standing up and stretching. "I'll have the boat ready and meet you at the pier in Santa Monica. You know where I dock."

"I know."

He asked me a final question: "What if you run into Tony Richetti when you're aboard the *Lady?*"

"If I do," I said quietly, "I'll kill him."

When I got back to my house in Pacific Palisades, Buddy told me he'd run out of candy for the neighborhood kids when they came Trick-or-Treating. A couple of them had thrown tomatoes at a front window and there was a real mess on the glass.

"Waste of good food, those tomatoes," he growled in his soft Haitian French accent. "In Haiti, no one is stupid enough to waste food. Not even little children."

"When I was young I did worse things than throw tomatoes. Get to sleep, Buddy. You look bushed."

"Night, Chief," he said, heading for his upstairs bedroom.

"I'll need a ride out to Santa Monica before dawn," I called after him. "I'll wake you up in time."

He gave me a wave and was gone.

I decided to phone Ray Chandler and tell him I was off *Blood Roads*. He picked up on the first ring and I gave him the news about Ernie Bulow.

"Will I still get my two thousand?"

"Sure," I said. "I'll mail you a check."

"Don't bother. Just bring it along with you to Santa Monica tonight."

"How did you—"

"Erle phoned me right after you left his place to tell me what the two of you are up to. I'm going along."

"The hell you are!" I was taut with anger. "Erle had no goddamn business telling you about this. In fact, why *did* he tell you?"

"He called to ask about one of my stories in *Mask*," said Chandler. "Wanted to make sure he wasn't stealing from me. His latest yarn has a similar plot, but once he outlined it, I told him to go ahead and write his version. There's no real carryover."

"What has all this crap to do with Santa Monica?"

"We got to gabbing and he mentioned that you'd been over to see him. One thing led to another and he told me about Shaw's daughter and the Cat's Eye and the whole business with Richetti. So I said I wanted to go along."

"Erle has a big mouth and you're nuts," I snapped. "The only reason I'm taking *him* is because it's his lousy boat. Otherwise, I'd go alone."

"Well, I'm tired of sitting on my bum in front of a typewriter," Ray said. "I'm going on this trip whether you like it or not. Been getting soft. I need a little excitement in my life."

"You could get yourself killed!"

53

"Oh, no. You'll be the one who buys it if anything goes wrong. I'll just be along for the ride."

"Damn it, Ray, you're one determined son of a bitch."

"I'm well aware of that," he said in his British accent. "See you in Santa Monica."

And I heard him chuckle before he hung up.

SIX

Buddy drove me to the pier, blinking sleep out of his eyes for most of the trip. When we got there I told him not to wait. I knew Ray would have his Duesy and could drive me back to the Palisades, so I told Buddy to go home and hit the sack.

"Okay, but you take care now, Chief," he said. "I worry about you."

He didn't know what I planned to do, but he made it a habit to worry about me anyway. Like an agitated mother hen.

"You ought to quit driving me around, find a good woman, get married, and raise a flock of kids," I told him. "Then you could worry about *them*."

"One of these days I might do just that." Buddy has a long face, like comedian Stan Laurel, with the same dopey smile. He gave me one of these smiles as he put the car in gear.

And, with a whisper of tires on night-damp pavement, the big limo rolled back into darkness.

I walked toward the area where Erle docked the *Blue Belle*. She was easy to spot—a sleek 38-footer painted sky-blue with her varnished deck wood gleaming under the overhead lights. I could see Gardner in the stern, coiling an anchor rope, wearing a long-billed cap and a heavy black cable-knit sweater. I had on a checked Mackinaw with the .38 snugged under my left armpit in its waterproof holster.

Erle saw me and waved as I crossed a short wooden boarding ramp to join him on deck.

"You're early," he said.

"That's fine. I don't mind us getting out there a little ahead of time. Besides, if we leave now we won't have to take Chandler with us."

"Too late," grinned Erle. "Here comes the Dulwich Kid now."

Chandler almost fell off the ramp as he crossed over. I remember he told me once that he had poor night vision, but that was bull; he just wasn't a very graceful guy. He was bundled up like an Eskimo, in thick mittens, storm coat, fur cap, and earmuffs. Ray hated chilly weather and it could get pretty cold on the ocean in the late night and early morning. But in that outfit he could have been warm at the North Pole.

"Crewman Chandler reporting aboard," he said, saluting us both.

"Ray, you're nuts," I said.

"You told me that on the phone. Actually, I'd be nuts to miss this caper. Maybe I'll get a story out of it. Dark, brooding night waters. Three intrepid adventurers stalking the lair of a dangerous killer. A beautiful girl's life at stake. It's got all the elements."

"Truth is stranger than fiction," I said.

"Not the way I write it," Ray countered. He turned toward Erle. "And when do we embark on our high seas escapade?"

"As soon as I run a final check on the engines," Gardner said.

"Engines?" I raised an eyebrow. "You have more than one?"

"The *Belle* is twin-screw and diesel powered," he said. "A seventy-five horsepower Chrysler does all the heavy work, but it's backed up by a forty horsepower Lycoming. I use it mostly for trolling, but if the Chrysler should conk out we can make shore with no problem on the Lycoming."

Chandler was impressed. "How much did this rig set you back? If you don't mind my asking."

"A shade over eight thousand, and that's a bargain for what she's got. Has her own galley and head, and her forward cabin sleeps six."

"How fast?" asked Ray.

"She'll do sixteen knots in a flat sea," Gardner replied with pride. "And she handles like a dream."

"Shaw would love this baby," declared Ray. "He's a real salt water freak."

"Yeah, someday I'll have Joe out here and take him fishing."

"Right now we're fishing for his daughter," I reminded Erle. "You'd better check those engines."

"Won't be long," he said.

While he was doing that I took an envelope out of my pocket and gave it to Chandler. "Your end of the script."

He opened it and noted that the check was written for three thousand, not the two we'd agreed on. After what Bulow had said, I felt I owed Ray the extra grand. And what the hell, it was only money.

"Thanks, Dash. No wonder you quit writing for Mask!"

"You ought to try some screen work on your own," I told him. "I've got plenty of connections around town. I could fix you up."

"Skip it," he said. "I can write scripts only when I'm drunk. I'm still feeling the hangover from Blood Roads."

"But you're a natural. Those twenty pages were dynamite."

"Look, my friend, prose is more honest, with no studio lamebrain telling you what has to go on the page."

He was right, of course. My best novels and stories for Shaw had given me something I never got out of scripting—gut satis-faction. Nothing I'd done for the silver screen even came close. Still, I'm basically a lazy fellow and I happen to require the things that the good life provides. Hollywood pays the kind of money I need.

By now, the Chrysler was throbbing smoothly as Erle came back to tell us that everything was jake. "She's ready to go," he said. "Dash, you cast off the bow line while I take us out. Ray, you handle the stern line."

Gardner mounted some steps to the flying bridge to take wheel. He gave us the high sign and we loosed the mooring ropes. The Chrysler increased power.

We were underway. Moving, one might say, into the jaws of the lion.

When we reached our stakeout area, dawn was just breaking. We could see broken patches of eastern sky through the pre-dawn fog as the darkness slowly gave way to a tinting of somber gray like smudged charcoal.

The Wicked Lady was riding high in the water a few hundred yards to port, with the night's last ship-to-shore motor launch anchored beside her, ready to transport the final load of gam-blers back to the pier in Santa Monica.

It was cold. I had the collar of my Mackinaw turned up as I felt the chill biting into my skin. "Won't be long now," I said. "With the gambling shut down, the crew will head for their bunks. Richetti will have a couple of guards posted, but they won't be expecting me. Once I'm aboard, it should be a cinch reaching his stateroom."

"Are you just saying this to make it sound easy?" Chandler asked me. "All it takes is one crewman to spot you and sound the alarm. Then your fat's in the fire."

"Colorfully put," I said. "But I'll make sure I'm not spotted."

"And even if you *do* manage to reach Richetti's private cabin

area, how are you going to find out if Shaw's daughter is still alive in there?"

"Trust me, Ray, if she's alive, I'll find her." The truth was I didn't really know *what* I'd do once I got to Richetti's cabin. It could be I'd get lucky and hear Clare's voice. But, then again, I'd never heard her speak. Maybe I could isolate one of the crew and force the truth about Clare out of him. I'd just have to wing it.

"At least you'll be spared having to swim over and back," Erle told me. "There's an inflatable rubber dinghy on board. You can use that."

"And leave it tied to the side of the ship?"

"Why not? The fog will make it tough to see anything from deck level."

"Thanks, Erle. I wasn't really looking forward to a swim. I know just how cold this damn water can get."

I eased the .38 out of its holster to check the load. I'd checked it earlier, but I was nervous: a reflex action.

"I hate those things," Ray muttered. "They're designed to kill people."

"I was a Pinkerton for seven years," I told him. "Carried a gun most of the time, but I never killed anybody with it. A boozed-up mug in Butte came at me once with a nine-millimeter Luger and I had to put a round in his right leg to slow him down. Shattered his kneecap. Very painful. You never want to get shot in the kneecap."

"Did you Pinkertons always carry weapons?" Erle asked.

"Not always. It depended on the case. You took along what the situation called for. One op I knew named Haultain used to pack *two* guns. A .45 automatic in a shoulder holster and a .38 in his coat. We'd enter a trouble area and Haultain would keep one hand in his pocket. If things heated up, and he didn't have time to go for the shoulder gun, he'd just tip up the .38 and fire right through the pocket."

"You can ruin a lot of coats doing that," said Gardner.

"Guns depress me," Ray declared. He stared at the .38 as I slipped it back into its holster.

"Strictly self-protection. I'd hate to be on Richetti's turf without it."

"I've done quite a bit of target practice," said Gardner. "Turns out I'm pretty good at it—but then I've never had to shoot at people."

"It's no fun," I said.

"I detest guns," declared Chandler. "A despicable human invention."

Erle grinned at him. "What about your stuff in *Mask?* You have your characters blasting away at each other like crazy."

"That's fiction. I may *write* about guns, but I'd never use one."

"I know you were in the war," I said. "You must have used weapons."

Chandler looked pained. "I was a platoon commander in France." He spoke softly. "I was forced to lead my men into direct machine-gun fire. Later, in our bunker, we suffered a particularly savage artillery attack. A shower of eleven-inch German shells. I was the only member of my unit to survive. Everyone else was killed." He hesitated for a long moment. "I've never fired a weapon since that day."

Erle and I didn't say anything. We could read the horror in his face. Ray had a good reason not to like guns.

By now we could see the passengers beginning to board the motor launch; the night's action was winding down on the *Lady.* I envisioned green dustcovers being stretched across baize tables, chips stacked and shelved, the roulette wheels motionless, and the last deck of playing cards torn and discarded.

Then: *Wham!* A sharp concussion rocked the ship, with a plume of smoke erupting from the forward section, followed by twisting fingers of flame, glowing pale yellow through the misting fog. We could hear passengers begin to scream. Then the ship's fire-alarm horn sent up its piercing wail.

"Jesus!" breathed Gardner. "What the hell's happened?"

"Some kind of explosion," I said. "It's a lucky break. With all the confusion aboard the *Lady*, I'll have a clear shot at finding Clare."

"*We'll* have," put in Chandler, as Erle broke out the rubber dinghy. "I'm going with you." He held up a mittened hand. "And don't tell me I'm nuts."

I glared at him. "Give me one good reason why I should take you along."

"The fire. We don't know how bad it is. It could spread fast. With your original plan, if you found Clare alive, you were going to leave her there and notify the Coast Guard. You can't do that now. Besides, what if Richetti kills her in the meantime?"

"I've thought about it," I admitted, "but I still haven't heard a reason why you should go with me."

"To help get Clare off the ship!" he said. His tone was intense. "In all the confusion the fire is causing we'll have an excellent chance to escape with her. Oh, you may have to use that damned gun of yours and we might have to kick down a couple of doors to reach her, but if and when we *do* find Clare, you'll need help getting her back to the dinghy. She might be drugged. I can carry her while you lead the way with your .38. And we can get across faster with two of us rowing." He paused for breath. "Is that reason enough?"

"All right, dammit, there's no time to stand here and argue." I turned to Erle. "Keep the Chrysler revved up. We might have to move fast."

"Right," he said.

There was mass panic aboard the *Lady*. Passengers were knocking each other down in a frenzied attempt to reach the motor launch and we could see some of them actually diving overboard. Insane! Unless they were picked up by one of the ship's lifeboats they wouldn't last long in that freezing water. But they weren't my concern; Joe Shaw's daughter was my concern.

61

"Are you sure you're up to this?" I asked Ray.

"Just watch me," he said.

"Then let's do it."

Ray and I piled into the dinghy, fumbled with the short wooden oars, then began to row for the ship. It was awkward at first. The rubber craft was unstable and tricky to maneuver, but we soon got the hang of it and began making steady progress. It was cold on the ocean and the spray from our oars struck at my skin like chilled bullets, but now the Lady loomed just ahead of us.

When we reached the ship (with the passenger launch on the opposite side), it towered above us like a New York skyscraper. Trying to climb up that sheer face was impossible, so we rowed along the hull until we located a boarding ladder. For supplies, most likely. Dropping anchor, we scrambled upward.

Topside, we were able to step onto the deck without attracting any attention. A few squealing passengers scurried by, but no crew members were in sight; by now they were all clustered at the bow, fighting to keep the fire from spreading. For all I knew, Tony boy himself was with them, shouting orders. The last thing he wanted was to see his ship go up in smoke.

We located the stairs and headed for the below-deck cabins. I had the .38 out of its holster and in my right hand and I was prepared to use it, but we had a clean run all the way to Richetti's stateroom suite. A few drunken, dazed-looking gamblers reeled down the corridor, ignoring us, and the one crew member who ran past us gripping a fire ax didn't even glance in our direction.

"This is great," nodded Chandler. "Really gets the old adrenaline pumping."

We were at the door of Richetti's stateroom, the same place I'd been taken to under guard the first night I was on the ship. I recognized the ornately carved dark oak door with its polished brass fittings.

I put my ear against the wood. Nothing. Silence.

"Do we kick it in?" asked Erle.

"There's a rule in the detective business: Never break down an unlocked door. And this one," I said, turning the brass knob, "is open."

I pushed Ray to one side, out of the direct line of fire, and brought up the .38 as the heavy oak door swung inward. No matter what was going on topside, the room might contain any number of posted guards, especially if Clare was being held captive here. In a half-crouch, I entered Tony Richetti's plush stateroom with Chandler right behind me.

The place was deserted.

"Nothing," said Ray.

"Let's check the back bedroom area," I said. "She could be locked in there."

As we started to cross the room I caught the strong odor of cordite in the air—and of fresh blood. Then I saw the heel of a man's shoe and quickly circled the desk.

There they were: Richetti and Clare, lying face down on the rug. I rolled them over.

"Christ!" said Chandler softly. "They've been shot to pieces!"

"We were too late," I said. "God! Poor Joe!" I checked the bodies. "Submachine gun. Whoever pulled off this job obviously set up the explosion and fire on deck to mask the gunfire."

I opened Richetti's blood-soaked coat and removed his wallet from an inside pocket. Flipped it open. It was stuffed with cash. Clare's purse was under the desk. I found her ID: Clare Vanikis, 2150 Colorado Boulevard, Pasadena, California.

I stood up. "Well, the killer sure wasn't after money. He even left Clare's ring on her finger."

It was the same antique emerald job I'd seen in the photo Joe had shown me back in New York. She wore it on her right hand,

and there was blood on her fingers. Clare's jet-black hair spilled across her bullet-ravaged face and her brown eyes were open, blank and staring. Sorry, Joe, I'm real, real sorry.

"If the killer wasn't after money," put in Chandler, "then what *was* he after?"

"This," I said. There was a square leather case on the desk—the same case I'd carried across country on the train. I gestured to Ray. "Open it."

He did.

Naturally, it was empty.

A thorough perusal of Richetti's desk and locked file cabinets would have linked him directly to a lot of dirt in Los Angeles, but there was no time for this. By now, in response to the fire, Coast Guard boats would be on the way and I didn't want them to find us in Richetti's stateroom.

"We have to get out," I told Ray, who had been snooping around the cabin.

He smiled at me, holding up a glittery object. "Look what I found behind the couch."

He tossed it over. A gold cigarette lighter, bearing three initials engraved inside a silver horseshoe design:

W P K

"Mr. Holmes," I said to him, "you have come up with a major clue."

"Well, Watson, what do you make of it?"

"WPK, I wager, stands for William Patrick Kelly."

"Big Bill?"

"Right."

"Owner of *The Lucky Horseshoe?*"

"Right again."

Kelly had been Richetti's chief competitor, running his own gambling ship off Santa Monica since 1930. They were bitter rivals. Over the past five years there had been killings on both sides, but nothing the Coast Guard cared to investigate. Somehow, Kelly had found out about the Cat's Eye, that Richetti had it aboard the *Lady*, and had acted promptly to obtain the treasure for himself.

"Looks like the case is solved," Ray said. "Kelly's our boy."

"Fine," I said. "And since he owns as much law as Richetti did, nobody's going to touch him. The papers and the radio will set up a howl about murder on the high seas, but nothing will come of it. Kelly has zero to worry about and he knows it."

"He has *us* to worry about."

"What's that supposed to mean?"

"Kelly's got the skull. It belongs to Shaw. We'll have to get it back."

"We came for Clare, remember? Now she's dead. That ends it."

He looked stunned. "You're just going to let Kelly keep the Cat's Eye?"

"Damn right I am! It's one thing to go risking my neck for Joe's kid, but it's something else again to risk it for his family treasure. We're writers, Chandler, not knights in shining armor. As far as I'm concerned, this case is closed."

He sighed. "Okay, I see your point."

"Then let's get out of here before we have the Coast Guard up our ass."

I did one final thing before we left. I removed the emerald ring from Clare's bloody finger.

Joe deserved to have it.

SEVEN

The afternoon papers were full of the story, with bold headlines about a DOUBLE HOMICIDE on board the *Lady* and how a "mystery fire" had been set to mask the killings. Splashed right under the lead story in the *Times* was a photo of Anthony R. Richetti labeled MURDERED GAMBLING CZAR. Tony was wearing a diamond stickpin as big as a hen's egg and looked very rich and self-satisfied.

There was also a fuzzy picture of Clare. They left the "i" out of her last name, spelling it "Vankis" instead of Vanikis. Naturally, they didn't connect her with Sylvia Vane, nor was there any mention of the Cat's Eye or of Big Bill Kelly.

The story did mention that three people had been lost at sea: two men and a woman who had panic-jumped from the upper deck. The men had not been identified, but the name of the missing woman was Mae Tilford. Two other women who had also abandoned ship as a result of the fire had been rescued by the Coast Guard and were reported to be in "severe shock." Yeah. The whole set-up was a severe shock to a lot of people.

The Mayor issued a phony front-page statement to the effect that L.A. was well rid of Mr. Anthony Richetti. He went on with a lot of self-righteous stuff about how Tony was a prime contributor to the "moral decay of the community" and that he had earned an illicit fortune "preying on the innocent and the gullible." Hizzoner concluded by saying that Richetti had "received his just deserts" and would now have to "face Almighty God for eternal judgment." What a crock! Now that Richetti was dead meat on a coroner's slab, His Honor was anxious to separate himself from the man who'd been greasing his palm with liberal bribe money.

I fingered Kelly's gold cigarette lighter in my coat pocket. Even if I *had* turned it over to the law they wouldn't have followed up on the investigation. The last thing the cops wanted to do was ruffle Kelly's feathers.

Not that I gave a damn about Big Bill Kelly. It was the Cat's Eye I wanted. But trying to go after it at this point in the game would be useless. There was no way to get to Kelly directly and even if I could, the Cat's Eye would be long gone by now. Probably on a boat to Europe. My guess was he'd be in contact with some money-fat private collectors over there and unload it for some very heavy green.

Any way you cut it, the Eye was gone—which is what I told Joe Shaw when I was finally able to reach him again in New York. I'd called him hours earlier, as soon as we got back to shore, to tell him Clare was dead, but he'd been so distraught at the bad news that he'd cut me off and hung up. When I called back, his secretary told me he'd gone home. I tried several times to get through, but he'd never answered his phone. Until now.

"I don't care about the Cat's Eye anymore," he said in a low, broken voice. "That damn thing cost my daughter's life. What I *do* care about is nailing the bastard who killed her."

"You mean you'd like Kelly's head on a plate." I'd told Joe about finding the lighter with Big Bill's initials on it.

"He's got to pay for what he did to Clare." Joe's voice rang over the long-distance wire. "That rotten piece of lizard shit can't get away with—"

"Hey!" I said, cutting into the flow. "It's just not going to happen. Kelly is a hundred percent cop-proof."

"You could nail him—by taking the lighter straight to the *Times*," he declared. "Make a public issue out of it. Then the police would be *forced* to arrest him."

"For what? The lighter could have been left in the cabin a long time ago, at some prior meeting between Richetti and Kelly. There's no way to prove it was dropped there on the night of the killing."

"But *you* believe that, don't you?"

"Okay, sure I do. But who cares what a burned-out screen hack believes? They'd laugh in my face. I know it hurts, but you're going to have to forget Kelly. He's in the clear."

"Not if you go after him," Shaw declared. "You're an ex-Pinkerton. You could use your detective training and figure out a way to nail this bastard."

"That's crazy, Joe. I'm out of this. I not only delivered the gizmo as promised, but got slugged for doing it. Then I made the attempt to get your daughter away from Tony. I was too late, and I'm sorry about that—but at least I tried. Sylvia and Clare are dead and there's nothing you or I can do about it."

"You could nail him, Dash. I *know* you could nail him."

"Forget it," I said. "It's finished. I'll talk to you later."

And I broke the connection.

After I put down the phone I felt like a heel. Joe had lost his only child and I'd played tough. But what else could I have said to him? The Pinkerton days were over. Going after Kelly as some kind of personal revenge on Shaw's behalf would be an act of insanity.

I'd told Joe the truth.

Luckily, I was out of it with my life. If Ray and I had crashed that cabin a few minutes earlier we'd have joined Tony and Clare. WRITERS ALSO SLAIN, the papers would have said. With our photos on page two next to the weather report.

Joe wasn't thinking straight. Once the shock of Clare's death wore off he'd realize he was asking me to do the impossible.

Just as I'd told him—it was finished.

But of course it wasn't.

That weekend Ben Hecht invited me to a party at Turkey Hill, which is what he calls his big wooden castle above Hollywood. Ben had been hot in the industry since 1927 when he'd been involved in the first popular gangster film, *Underworld*. I met him after he'd adapted one of my stories for the screen as *Roadhouse Nights* (not that he used much of my plot). We hit it off right away. Had a lot in common. He'd been a Chicago newspaper man during the Capone era. He'd ask me about my experiences with the Pinks and I'd ask him about the gang days in Chicago. Birds of a feather.

Most Hollywood parties are a bore. Dull people, half-sloshed, standing around with drinks in their hands, trying to impress other dull people. But Ben knew how to throw a wingding. He always attracted individuals with talent and wit—and he knew everybody who was anybody in the industry.

When I arrived at Turkey Hill there were at least two dozen wild turkeys wandering the lawn. Ben never bothered to explain why he kept these birds around and I never asked. I don't think he ever cooked one; they were probably all pals of his. Hecht had a lot of odd quirks.

I passed the huge mosaic fountain bubbling away like Vesuvius on the front terrace and walked into Ben's castle. As usual, the door was wide open; he didn't believe in locks.

Charles MacArthur, Ben's hard-drinking collaborator, had passed out on the hallway floor and I had to step over him to get to the main drawing room where the party was going full blast. The place was big enough to play football in, jammed to the rafters with Hollywood's elite. Harpo Marx was head-to-head with Groucho over a game of checkers in front of the wide stone fireplace. George Raft was in a heated argument with Jimmy Durante at the corner wall bar, and Tallulah Bankhead was dancing on top of the piano with a long-stemmed red rose in one hand and an empty martini glass in the other.

A typical Hecht blowout.

I headed for Ben who was trying to talk Bill Powell into taking the lead in a new Hecht screenplay. "If you tell Mayer you want to do it he'll greenlight the picture," Ben was saying as I walked up to them.

"You trying to hustle my star?" I asked Hecht, who looked like a nervous bulldog. He wore a suit that must have looked great in Chicago but just didn't play in L.A. Powell was his usual dapper self, cool and collected. He'd scored big as my detective Nick Charles in *The Thin Man*. I'd written a nifty 115-page sequel for M-G-M about the same characters, and Powell was again set to play Nick to Myrna Loy's Nora.

"Stay out of this, Hammett," Ben growled in mock anger. "Bill and I are about to come to an artistic agreement."

"Good to see you, Dash," Powell said, shaking my hand firmly. He nodded toward Ben. "There's only one reason why I won't promote your friend's screenplay."

"What's the reason?" I asked him.

He gave me a sardonic smile. "It stinks."

Ben didn't even blink. Veteran of a thousand slings and arrows, he bounced back with: "I guarantee you'll *love* the next one I send you."

"I can hardly wait," Powell said, and drifted away into the crowd.

"Smug son of a bitch," muttered Ben. Then he asked me what I'd have to drink, easing me toward the corner bar.

"Johnny Walker with soda," I said. "Heavy on the soda. I'm trying to stay sober these days."

"A laudable goal, but an unlikely one," said Ben, mixing my drink. "All good writers are alcoholics."

I thought of Hemingway and Fitzgerald and big Tom Wolfe and didn't argue the point.

"Besides," Ben went on, "you always tell your best stories when you're drunk. Remember the one you told us at my last party—about the gun duel you had with a dope-crazed kid in the middle of Market Street at high noon? That was a real peach."

"There wasn't any duel," I said. "He was so hopped up he couldn't shoot straight. When his gun was empty I just walked up and took it away from him."

"I like the drunk version better," Hecht said, handing me my drink.

He'd fixed a gin rickey for himself and after taking a swig asked me if I knew anything about the double killing aboard the *Lady*.

"Only what I read in the papers."

"Got any ideas as to who might have done the job?"

"Nope," I said. "But whoever it was used up a lot of machine-gun bullets."

"Yeah." Ben nodded. "Richetti and the girl were really perforated. Reminds me of the old days in Chicago."

I'd come to Ben's party to get my mind off murder, so I changed the subject. "I hear you're writing a picture for Lombard and Freddie March."

"Right," he said. "A comedy, *Nothing Sacred*. Oscar Levant's supposed to do the music, and Wellman might direct. But it's at least a year away from production, so who knows? I'm only half through the second draft."

Then, despite myself, I couldn't help asking: "You know Big Bill Kelly?"

"Sure," Ben nodded quickly. "Almost lost my shirt at craps last time I was on his boat."

"He ever been here—to Turkey Hill?"

"Nah," he said. "I don't invite his kind to my shindigs. Kelly would drag along half a dozen muscle boys and they'd spoil the fun."

"But you do know him personally, as a friend?"

"Not as a friend, for Christ's sake!" declared Hecht. "Kelly's only friend is his wallet. Guy lives for money." He chuckled. "And for sex. Hear tell he'll screw anything that can breathe, male or female. But don't quote me on it."

"Who's he been screwing lately?"

"Jeez, how should I know? Go ask Louella Parsons." He blinked at me. "How come you're so hot for info on Bill Kelly?"

I shrugged. "You know I'm always keen on the bad boys," I said. "Kelly interests me. He carries a lot of weight in L.A."

"He's not in the same league with Al Capone," Ben declared. Hecht had been one of the writers on the Muni pic, *Scarface*, and he knew a lot about the legendary Chicago gang boss. "I could write a book on Capone."

"Then why don't you?"

"I've been considering it—putting in all the stuff I had to leave out of *Scarface*."

I felt a hand tap my left shoulder and a female voice behind me rasped: "Dash, you handsome bastard, how they hangin'?"

It was Dorothy Parker. She had some kind of literary crush on me. The first time we met, at a cocktail party in New York, she'd dropped to her knees in front of me and kissed my hand. It was damned embarrassing. At the time she'd mumbled something about how I wrote better women than any male author in America. Lily thought she was funny, but I'd never liked her. Not then, not now.

"Hello, Dotty," I said, hoping she wouldn't drop to her knees.

She was wearing a dress with too many sequins on it and her dark eyes were crazy.

"I'm drunk," she said. "Are you drunk?"

"No."

"Well, I'm soused to the bloody gills." She pointed at Hecht. "On Ben's whiskey."

"What am I supposed to say to that?" I asked.

"Not a goddam thing, sweetie," she said. "I just wanted to come over and tell you that I hate your guts."

I smiled. "Thought you had me pegged as the great white hope of American letters."

"That's why I hate you." She was small, short-haired, mannish. I guess some men find her type attractive.

"You're a sellout. I read that lousy comic thing of yours in the paper and I wouldn't wrap a dead fish in it."

She meant *Secret Agent X-9*, the newspaper strip I'd written for King Features. "I gave that up a while back," I said. "I'm doing films now."

"Piss on films. How come you're not doing another mystery novel? Sam Spade. God, how I love that man! Why aren't you doing another Sam Spade?"

"Because I've said all I want to say in that format. *The Thin Man* did it for me." I didn't owe her any explanations, but I was feeling charitable. After all, she *was* a good pal to Lily.

"You're full of crap," she said. Then she punched me in the chest, giggling. "But then, you've *always* been full of crap."

"And you're full of booze," I said.

"That I am, that I am." Her body swayed. " 'Scuse me, darlin', I have to go puke."

And she tottered off toward the nearest head.

"Dotty's a real character," said Hecht, who'd silently observed our little exchange. "She really admires you, Dash."

"She's a spoiled, sharp-tongued bitch," I said. "People let her get away with murder because they think she's clever."

"Maybe she hit a sore spot with you."

"What's that supposed to mean?"

"About your not writing novels anymore."

"What I write or don't write is my damn business." I glared at him. "And I don't like people butting into my damn business."

"Hey, forget I ever mentioned it!"

But of course Ben was dead center. I *knew* I had to get to work on another book. I went home that night and indulged myself by brooding about it.

Which was better than brooding about Big Bill Kelly.

I couldn't sleep that night so, after ice cream sodas, Buddy and I played Ping-Pong in the rumpus room. We're fairly matched, which means good volleys. And when you're into a good volley, you can't think about anything else, so I finally stopped brooding.

We'd just finished a game when he glanced at me with a sly grin. "You know who killed Tony Richetti and the woman, don't you, Chief?"

That startled me. But Buddy often startles me with his uncanny intuitions. His Haitian voodoo, I figure.

"I have a pretty fair idea."

"You're not going to do anything about it?"

"No, I'm not."

"You're feeling guilty." It was a flat statement.

"What are you, my psychiatrist?"

"I know you, Chief. You're feeling guilty over not doing anything about a killer."

"That's not my job anymore," I said. "I've been a long time out of the detective game."

"It's in your blood."

I put down the wooden paddle and moved away from the table. "I'm going to bed."

"Sweet dreams," said Buddy.

"I'll try to have some," I said.

EIGHT

I decided that the best way to get my mind off Bill Kelly was to bury myself in another script job, so now that I was free of my Global contract, I accepted an offer from Universal to write an original story about a young, handsome private eye who is really a heel. A switch on the standard hero detective theme and one I thought might have some juice.

Writing it turned out to be fun and it kept me out of trouble for a month.

I called my guy "Gene Raymond" (after Chandler) and had him involved in a case of murder and blackmail centering around a wealthy stockbroker name Pomeroy. Raymond meets Ann, the stockbroker's twenty-year-old daughter, and she thinks he's an on-the-square detective. Actually, he's in cahoots with the blackmailer. At the climax, he loses Ann to Joe King, a narco officer who exposes Raymond and the blackmailer. There's a chase and a mountain shootout where King kills Raymond and drives off into the sunset with Ann Pomeroy. I titled it *On the Make*.

My producer at Universal, a wispy little gink in granny glasses named Billy Berna, called me in for a story conference after

76

reading my first draft. He paced the office the way a captive animal circles its cage, trailing cheap cigar smoke and looking miserable. I've noticed that most producers smoke cigars and look miserable. They worry about a lot of things. At the moment, Billy was worried about the relationship between Ann and Joe King. He stabbed the air with his cigar when he talked to me.

"Cripes, Dash, they don't even *meet* each other until the story's half over," he whined, scrubbing at his veined nose with a manicured fingernail. "That's not the way a romance works, kiddo. The build-up has gotta be *gradual*—what I like to call orchestrated emotion."

"Nice phrase," I said.

"See, kiddo, we have to make our audience *believe* in this relationship. Meaning we orchestrate it—like you build a concerto. Like that Beethoven guy. You *build*."

"Uh-huh," I said. "So what do you suggest?" I stifled a yawn.

Berna glared at me over his glasses. "Are you, by any chance, *bored* by what I've been saying?"

"Maybe a little," I admitted.

He stopped pacing to face me. His cigar smelled like sour cheese. "It seems obvious to me that you're a victim of a staggering sense of self-destruction."

"What I'm a victim of, Billy," I said pleasantly, "is having to work for a dimwit like you."

"That cuts it," he snapped, tossing me my outline. He turned his back. "Get out, Hammett."

I got out.

Shoot, boy, I told myself as I walked toward the studio gate, you've done it again. Got yourself fired from another plum job with your smartass mouth. Ray Chandler was right when he told me: "You're one of those guys who can't take Hollywood on its own terms. You're always in there, trying to push God out of the high seat."

And that afternoon at Universal, Billy Berna happened to be God.

The Berna meeting would, for certain, have ended up in the personal Hammett disaster column except for Charly.

A her, not a him. Very definitely female. Tall, full-figured, red-haired. With a cat's green eyes. And obviously attracted to self-destructive screen writers. I met her at the gate when she overheard me asking the guard to call a taxi, it being Buddy's day off.

"Need a ride?" she asked in a tone that reminded me of rippling silk. She was behind the wheel of a red Auburn roadster (to match her hair?) and if she wore any makeup I couldn't spot it. Her lips were pale and full and looked fine that way. She'd poured herself into a neatly curved rust-colored outfit that accented her freckles.

"I was calling for a taxi," I said.

"Forget it. I can take you where you want to go, Mr. Hammett."

"I'll bet you can," I said, grinning at her as I climbed into the Auburn's mohair seat. "How'd you know my name?"

She put the roadster into gear and we motored briskly down Lankershim Boulevard. "*The Thin Man* has your picture on it."

"I hope you did more than look at the cover. You did read the book, right?"

"Every page. It was wonderful. Made me homesick for Christmas in New York."

Whenever anyone mentions *The Thin Man* out here in Hollywood I always figure they're talking about the movie. Readers are a rare breed, and I told her so.

"I've been reading since I was old enough to hold a book. Dad encouraged me. He was a grade school teacher in Brooklyn."

"I used to haunt the library in Baltimore when I was a kid," I told her. "Read my first mystery there."

"I have all your books," she said. "Just loved Casper Gutman in *Falcon*. I was rooting for him to find the Black Bird." She flashed me a terrific smile. "I'm a big fan of yours."

"That's nice," I said, meaning it.

"Are you married?" she asked me.

"Not at the moment."

"Great. Then we can go to bed together."

That was Charly. Totally direct. No romantic buildup for her. Billy Berna wouldn't have approved. She obviously wasn't into orchestrated emotion.

We drove to her place—a small pink stucco apartment facing an open court on Franklin near Gower. It was neat and clean inside, with several large film posters of Clark Gable tacked to the walls.

"I adore him," she said, walking over to the one featuring Gable and Harlow in *Red Dust*. She ran her hand over the actor's face. "He has a delicious mustache. Like you do. Facial hair is so masculine."

"Are you an actress?" I asked her as she slipped out of her jacket. Her breasts were perfect under a tight emerald sweater that matched her eyes.

"I work in the sound department at Universal," she told me. "My boyfriend got me the job before he dropped me for a blonde secretary at RKO. I hate blondes."

"Sorry," I said.

"That I hate blondes?"

"No, that you lost your boyfriend."

"Well, *don't* be. He was an A-1 creep. He'd get mean and slap me around. Beat me so bad last month that I almost lost a tooth."

"Then I'd say you're well rid of him."

"Besides. . . ." And she gave me an impish smile. "He didn't have a mustache."

* * *

She was good in bed. We made love on her pulldown under a poster of Gable and Colbert in *It Happened One Night*. With us, it happened in the afternoon.

It was when we'd finished and she was relaxing with her head against my bare chest that she told me all her friends call her Charly. "My full name is Charlene Frances Maddix, but I always hated being called Charlene."

"My full name is Samuel Dashiell Hammett," I said, "but I always hated being called Samuel."

She giggled. "Dash fits you."

"And Charly fits you."

"I'm glad you don't wear an undershirt," she told me, running her fingers through my chest hair. "When Gable took off his clothes in *It Happened One Night*, he was bare-chested. I really liked that."

"Do you always go to bed with the men you see on book jackets?" I asked her.

"Oh, no! I'm a very moral person. It's just that power excites me. Sexually. And your books are very powerful."

"I've never thought of them that way."

"I love it at the end of *Falcon* where Sam tells Brigid he's not going to play the sap for her, that although she may love him and he may love her, he's turning her over to the cops. She's got to take the fall for what she did to his partner. That was *very* powerful."

"It was a tough scene to bring off," I said. "To make it real. By then, he was stuck on her. But love doesn't cancel out murder. Sam was a detective and he had to play by the rules."

"Has a woman ever made a sap out of you?"

"Plenty of times," I admitted. "But then, I'm not Sam Spade. I'm not Nick Charles, either. Sometimes people get me mixed up with the characters I write about. I make them stronger and tougher and better than I am. Believe me, I'm no prize for any woman."

"I think you could get an argument going on that," she said. "For one thing, you're incredibly handsome."

"Facade," I grinned. "It's what's inside that counts." I was thinking about the fact that if I'd had more guts I would have gone after Bill Kelly. Spade would have gone after him. For sure.

"Have you ever been married?" she asked me.

"Yes. Once."

"I'm very curious about the type of woman you'd marry. Tell me about her."

And I did. I avoid talking to people about Jose and the early years when we were newly married in San Francisco, but this situation was different somehow. Maybe it was psychological. Maybe I needed to reconnect with my past and Charly just happened to press the right emotional button. I don't really know *why* I told her about our marriage, but I did. I told her.

"She's from Montana. Her name is Josephine Anna Dolan," I said, "but I called her Jose. We met at a hospital in Tacoma, Washington, when I was a lunger."

"What's a lunger?"

"I had tuberculosis. Jose was a nurse and she took care of me."

"Are you contagious?" There was concern in her tone.

"Oh, no. I cured the TB years ago. I'm talking 1920, and even then I wasn't all that sick. Jose was in her early twenties, with dark hair. Looked real cute in her nurse's cap. After my health improved we started going for walks together in the park. I guess you could say we fell in love, but love is a word I don't trust much. Too many people misuse it." I hesitated, remembering. "Anyhow, eventually we separated."

"What happened?"

"I was sent to an army hospital near San Diego and Jose was reassigned back to Montana. But by then she was pregnant."

"With *your* child?"

"Sure. She hadn't slept with anybody else. When I found out, I wrote her a letter asking her to marry me."

"Where were you married?"

"San Francisco. Summer of twenty-one. We rented a cheap downtown apartment, which was all we could afford. I was working for Pinkerton again, and I wasn't liking it much."

"Were you a good detective?"

"Well . . . I was a good shadow man."

"What's that?"

"I had a talent for shadowing suspects. I could follow them anywhere and they'd never spot me. But mostly the work was a grind. And that cold wet Frisco fog was murder on my lungs. I finally quit the game in twenty-two, the same year I began selling stories."

"How long did you stay in San Francisco?"

"Long enough."

"That's not an answer."

"Hey, Charly, I'm tired of talking about myself. No more questions, okay?"

"Can we talk about your novels?"

"No."

"Then what *can* we do?"

"I'll think of something," I said, my hand running smoothly up and down her thigh.

She giggled. "You never get tired of it, huh?"

"Remember, I said no more questions."

She leaned forward and softly kissed me on the lips.

Charly insisted on driving me back to my place in Pacific Palisades, but I didn't ask her inside. She'd been swell in bed, but all the talk about Jose had depressed me. I figured that what I needed most right now was to be left alone.

The phone was ringing when I walked in. It was my agent,

Leland Hayward, a very classy guy who understands writers. Most agents don't.

"This has got to stop, Dash."

"What's got to stop?"

"Getting yourself fired from the jobs I set up for you."

"I'll admit it's a bad habit."

"Billy Berna phoned. He was very upset. Apoplectic, to be precise. Said you grievously insulted him."

"That's an overstatement. I just told him he was boring me. Oh . . . I also called him a dimwit."

"For Christ's sake, Dash, you can't talk that way to a producer!"

"He had his head up his ass," I said. "I like to work for people I respect."

"Which eliminates about ninety-five percent of the producers in this town."

"So I'll work for the other five percent."

"I'm no bloody miracle man. You're making it really tough for me."

"Sorry about that, Leland, but it's my perverse nature."

"You could be big in this town if you'd just get off your damn high horse."

"You mean I could be a big sellout in this town. Dotty Parker thinks I'm one already."

A sigh on the other end of the line. "So what do you want me to do?"

"Get me another job with Rouben Mamoulian. I enjoyed doing City Streets for him. Rouben's a gentleman."

"He's tied up on a couple of new pictures, but I'll talk to him about you when he's open. Meantime, I'll look around for something you might like."

"Not something, somebody," I said. "I wrote a lot of crap for Joe Shaw because I liked him."

"That wasn't crap and you know it. Your *Mask* stuff will outlive us all."

"Be nice to think so, but I wouldn't lay odds on it."

"I'll be in touch," Leland said, and rang off.

I was in the mood for some mindless diversion so I poured myself a tall tumbler of tomato juice and sat down in the library to tune in Sherlock Holmes. The Great Man's "uncanny powers of deduction" never failed to amuse me as he solved cases by analyzing shreds of Turkish pipe tobacco or the leaf mold on a dead man's boot. Then there was his never-ending battle of wits with the Napoleon of crime, Professor Moriarty, once described over the air by Holmes (and I recall the exact words) as "the greatest schemer of all time, the organizer of every deviltry, the controlling brain of the underworld, a brain which might have made or marred the destiny of nations."

I'd never met a detective remotely like Mr. Holmes, nor had I encountered any Napoleons of crime in my years with Pinkerton. But that didn't keep me from enjoying the lurid adventures of the man from Baker Street.

On this particular night, as I adjusted the sound level on my Philco for the final episode of "The Curious Case of the Purloined Pearl," the Great Detective had just waylaid a hooded character packing a loaded horse pistol on the fog-shrouded moor surrounding Wheatshire House. Holmes caught the rascal as he was about to enter the mansion and, after a brief tussle, knocked him flat with the butt of his own weapon. Just as a badly winded Watson arrived, Holmes pulled off the man's hood.

"It's Sir Willard Wheatshire!" exclaimed the agitated doctor. "But why, in the name of heaven, would he be attempting to break into his *own* house?"

"I shall explain everything in due course, my good fellow, in due course," purred Holmes in a voice of calm assurance. "But first, a search through the pockets of his greatcoat is in order."

"And just what do you expect to find?"

"Patience, dear Watson, patience. Ah—*here* it is!"

"Great Scott, Holmes! It's the missing pearl—the legendary Blood Pearl of the Bonfidinis!"

"Ah—do not be deceived, Watson. I think you will find, under close examination, that this is a very clever *fake.*"

"Impossible! Why would Sir Willard carry a fake pearl to match the *real* one that was stolen from him?"

"Because the real pearl was *never stolen!*"

Watson sputtered. "But . . . but Holmes . . . that's the very reason we were called here—to recover it."

"True enough, but Sir Willard had been cleverly *duped* into believing that the blood pearl was missing."

"And it actually was not?"

"Correct, Watson. It was Lady Wheatshire who informed her husband that a fake pearl had been substituted for the heavily-guarded original—and he accepted her bold fabrication."

"Fabrication?"

"Precisely. In truth, my dear fellow, Lady Wheatshire has been working hand in glove with that infamous jewel thief, the Earl of Clax. Together, they invented a lurid story of theft, knowing that the so-called fake pearl would no longer be placed under house guard. After all, why would anyone guard a fake? Thus, the thief could quite easily enter the library and remove the *genuine* pearl, replacing it with this false one."

"Confound you, Holmes! I'm still in the dark on

this. If what you say is true, why would Sir Willard break into his own house to steal his own property?"

"A very sound and logical question," said Holmes smugly. "In truth he would not. But you see, Watson, this scurrilous rascal is *not* Sir Willard. He is wearing a very convincing face mask—which I shall now remove. Voila!"

"Great Scott! He's . . . he's the Earl of Clax!"

"Exactly so, Watson. Fortunately, I managed to waylay the scoundrel before he could enter Wheatshire House disguised as Sir Willard, alleviating all suspicion should he be seen inside. Upon reaching the library, our wily friend here intended to replace the *real* pearl with this carefully crafted fake."

"Incredible! Upon my word, Holmes, absolutely incredible!"

"Now all that remains is to appraise Inspector Lestrade of the full situation. He can then tender formal charges against Lady Wheatshire for her nefarious part in this dastardly affair."

"You are nothing short of amazing, Holmes! Simply amazing!"

"Tush and nonsense," said the Great Detective. "It's all elementary, my dear Watson."

Chuckling, I finished my tomato juice and switched off the radio. If only real-life crime were as easy to deal with! I was certain that old Sherlock would have no trouble sending Big Bill Kelly to the slammer and tracking down the missing Cat's Eye in the bargain. Elementary, my dear Hammett.

I was in the act of snapping off the standing lamp near the radio when I hesitated. I'd heard a sound from the outside hall. Someone was there.

Instinctively, I dived for the rug as a gun flashed and roared from the doorway. The slugs ripped past my head, but I groaned loudly as if I'd been hit, rolling over on my back. A dark figure, backlit by the hallway light, stepped into the library, gun extended.

As he walked toward me, moving cautiously, I played dead. I couldn't jump him with that lethal .45 in his hand, but when he got close enough. . . .

I grabbed his right ankle, twisting it violently. Off-balance, he lurched sideways, and before he could trigger the automatic again I was up and at him.

The guy was prize-ring material, big and burly, with muscles over his muscles, and my fists weren't doing much to him. He was swinging the .45 toward me and I knew in another split second I'd have a lead slug in my gut. That's when I grabbed a heavy iron poker from the fireplace and laid it across his skull. He staggered, falling back into a bookcase, shattering the glass doors.

But he wasn't done yet, so I tackled him again. The two of us wrestled for possession of the gun. A muffled explosion, and I felt him suddenly go limp in my arms. I let go and he slipped to the rug, blood flowing from his chest. Kneeling beside him, I took the big .45 from his shaking hand. "Who are you?"

"A . . . a pal of . . . of Tony's," he gasped. A froth of blood bubbled at his lips, which meant the bullet had penetrated a lung. He wasn't going to last long. "I . . . saw you . . . leaving the ship . . . figured you . . ."

"You figured I killed Tony Richetti, right?"

He nodded, coughing blood. "Me an' Tony . . . we were . . . real close . . . so I came here . . . to pay you back."

"*You're* the one who's dying," I said. "Too bad, pal, because I didn't have a damn thing to do with Richetti's gundown. You've wasted your life."

"I guess . . . I played it dumb." He fell silent, his eyes glazing over. His head rolled back and he was gone. I had a corpse on my library floor.

I did some thinking. What I *didn't* need was having to answer a lot of questions from the cops about how come this guy was shot and why he was in my house and what did I have to do with his death and maybe you'd just better come on down to the station with us, Mr. Hammett.

Luckily, Buddy hadn't arrived home yet from his night on the town. If I was careful, he'd never know anything about this. The dead man had fallen onto a throw rug which now had a lot of blood on it. I rolled his body into the rug, then cleaned up things in the library, planning to tell Buddy that I'd accidentally stumbled into the bookcase.

I dragged the dead punk out to the backyard. Then I got a shovel from the gardener's shack, dug a neat hole, and buried him, rug and all. It took some sweat, but at least I was rid of the problem.

That night I dreamed about making love to Sylvia Vane. We were reaching a mutual climax when Big Bill Kelly appeared in the bedroom door with a tommy gun. He told me I had a skinny ass.

Sylvia ran over to him, throwing her arms around his neck. "*You're* the one I really want," she said, thrusting her legendary tits against his chest.

Kelly grinned, pushing her back. "Hold your horses, sweetie, first I got to do a job on this shitty detective."

"You have me all wrong," I told him. "I'm no shitty detective. Haven't been for a long, long time. I'm a shitty screen writer."

But the big man cut loose on me with the Thompson and I felt the bullets chopping up my body. No pain. Just the dull wet smack of the machine-gun bullets entering my flesh, the cold impact of those heavy slugs, ripping me apart. . . .

NINE

The next morning I got a phone call from Erle. He needed to see me so I had Buddy drop me at his place. This time Gardner was in the main house, dressed in robe and pajamas. He met me at the door and we went into the living room. In direct contrast to his trailer, the place was uncluttered and neat as a pin. Probably the work of his Filipino houseboy.

Gardner looked hangdog. That was his expression, no other word for it. I sat down across from him.

"What's on your mind?" I asked. "You look terrible."

"I couldn't sleep last night," he said, "so I stayed up and dictated a complete Ed Jenkins novelette."

"Bully for you." There was a twinge of jealousy in my tone. "What kept you from sleeping?"

"Guilt."

"Over what?"

"Turning down Joe Shaw," Erle told me. "I talked to Joe yesterday and he asked me to use my skills as an ex-lawyer to help nail Bill Kelly."

"Yeah," I nodded. "He asked me to use *my* skills as an ex-detective to do the same thing."

"And you refused?"

"Damn right I refused. The evidence of Kelly's lighter is worthless."

"I told Joe the same thing. Said there was nothing either of us could do."

"You were right, there isn't."

"Anyway, I ended up feeling guilty as hell. Then, this morning, I got some information from a Chinese I know—a guy named Yin Shan. He owns a grocery store downtown."

"What kind of information did Shan give you?"

"It concerned an eyewitness."

I sat up straight, staring at him. "To the murders? You've tagged somebody who saw Kelly gun down Richetti and Clare?"

"I haven't tagged him yet," said Erle. "But if Shan is on track, then I know where we can look for him."

"We?"

"Sure. The two of us have to follow up on this as a team."

I let that one slide by for the moment to ask: "Where is this guy?"

"San Francisco. Holed up somewhere in Chinatown."

I grunted. "Tough place."

Memories flashed through my mind. Back in '26 I'd written a *Black Mask* story set in Chinatown, "Dead Yellow Women," based on a case I'd been involved in as a Pinkerton. At the time, I'd made a loyal friend there, Ching Hoo Lun, who ran a plush gambling club on Grant. All the top locals spent their money at Lun's joint. A tong clansman named Lim Mow accused Lun of cheating and vowed to kill him. Lun hired me as a bodyguard, and I saved his life when Mow tried to dice him with a carving knife. It was a close thing and I got the blade in my left thigh, which put me in the hospital.

When I wrote my yarn for *Mask*, Ching Hoo Lun became my villainous Chinatown biggie, Chang Li Ching. Lun got a big kick out of the published story. Insisted that I autograph the issue. In gratitude, he offered me the free services of a Chinese muscle-man to use if I ever wanted anybody worked over—a leg broken or a skull cracked, stuff like that. I never took advantage of the offer, but it was nice to know it was there.

Now I said to Erle: "People disappear in Chinatown all the time. They go in, but they don't come out. It's a separate world. Besides, how can you be sure this eyewitness is really there?"

"Shan knows these two Sing brothers, Wong and Wu. They were hired by Bill Kelly as manservants. Personal valets. Wong Sing told Shan that his brother was with Kelly on board the *Lady* the night of the shooting and that he quit the next day and lit out for Chinatown. Before he left, he gave Wong some kind of story about going up to Frisco to visit his parents, but Wong thinks Wu left because of what happened on the *Lady*."

I nodded. "So Wong figures that his brother saw the killings and got scared that Kelly wouldn't want him around as a living witness."

"Right, and he didn't cotton to being a dead one. So he took off for Frisco with the idea that Kelly could never find him in Chinatown. Needle in a Chinese haystack."

"Makes sense," I said. "I know the area. I think there's a good chance I can find him. But there's no use your getting involved."

"Wrong. You may know Chinatown, but you don't know the language. I do. And to find Wu Sing we're going to need to speak Cantonese."

I recalled Erle's law background in Oxnard. He'd handled all of the court cases for the Chinese community and they'd dubbed him *tai Chong tze*, the "big lawyer." He certainly knew their lingo. And he'd written about them, too. There was one Gardner story in *Mask* with the title set entirely in Chinese characters. Shaw hadn't wanted to run it that way, but Erle insisted. "The story's in English, so why can't the *title* be in Chinese?" And he won his case.

Erle was saying: "If Wu Sing *did* see Kelly use a tommy gun on Richetti and the girl, and he's willing to testify, then the L.A. cops will have no choice. They'll *have* to arrest Kelly and charge him with the murders."

"That's a big 'if.' Let's just suppose we get lucky and manage to find this guy. What makes you think he'll cooperate with us?"

"He'll want to put Kelly away to protect himself. According to his brother, most of the Sing family lives here in L.A. This is where he wants to be. So he's got a damn good reason to help convict Kelly."

"Well, then. . . ." I shrugged. "Looks like we're going to Chinatown."

It hadn't changed much in ten years. My last visit had been in late '25, when I was researching my story for Shaw, but all the sights, sounds, and smells were sharply familiar: the sea of chatter that Erle understood but I didn't, the chop suey joints with their strong odors of hot oil and spice and vinegar, the small family produce markets with wooden crates of fresh vegetables stacked along the street, the gaudy fan tan parlors, the "joy houses" filled with grinning Chinese sailors, the bustling garment shops and open bazaars, and the cloying sweet smell of jasmine incense drifting out of the green-roofed pagoda-style temples along Waverly Place.

Chinatown had spread out a little since I'd been here last, but the basic layout was the same, starting from the shopping district at California Street and extending north to the Latin Quarter. Grant Avenue was the main thoroughfare and it was always jammed and noisy.

There was a funeral procession on Grant the afternoon Erle and I arrived, marked by the strident blare of a marching street band. The family of the deceased, in solemn white, walked beside a horse-drawn hearse bearing the casket.

The principal characteristic of Chinese culture is devotion to family. It gets a little intense, and most wholesale killings result from family feuds. The bitter, bloody tong wars, with clan against clan, show just how seriously the Chinese value their families. Much earlier, when the tongs were going full blast, Chinatown was out of control, a literal hotbed of violence, vice, and corruption. Young Chinese girls were openly sold into slavery to fill the host of cribs and sweatshops lining the streets, and whether you were Chinese or not, it was worth your life to be here after dark.

With the funeral din fading behind us, we turned off Grant to Clay, then moved up Spofford Alley. Spofford houses a variety of family associations and social clubs in some very fancy buildings. One of the fanciest belonged to my influential Chinese friend, Ching Hoo Lun, who was up to his double chin in gambling enterprises, opium dens, and joy houses. In Chinatown, Lun was the man to see if you wanted info on who was hiding where. I was hoping we wouldn't need to utilize Erle's ability to speak Cantonese; maybe Lun would put his fat finger smack on Wu Sing's hideout. At least there was no problem in basic communication as Lun spoke excellent, if florid, English, just the way Chang Li Ching did in my story. I've made a practice of basing most of my fictional creations on real people. Most of the characters in *Falcon*, for example, have real-life originals.

Brigid O'Shaughnessy was based on a secretary named Peggy O'Toole who worked for me in San Francisco. Casper Gutman was a fat man I shadowed in Washington, suspected of being an enemy spy. Joel Cairo was a forger I'd arrested in 1920, and Wilmer, the gun-toting kid, was a small-time punk we caught robbing filling stations in Stockton.

My nameless Continental Op in *Red Harvest* and *The Dain Curse* was directly based on the Pinkerton man who trained me to be a detective, Jimmy Wright of Baltimore, a streetwise little bullet of a guy. I got the character of Babe McCloor—in my story "Fly Paper"—from Jimmie the Riveter's mob, a nasty bunch of yeggs we ran down in Seattle. McCloor was with them, and when we cornered him he made a dive for his gun and shot it out, cowboy style, right there in the street. Babe was one tough cookie. And, as I've said before, Nick's wife, Nora Charles, in *The Thin Man*, is really Lillian Hellman.

All good writers do this sort of thing. We rely on our lives, on our individual experiences and on the people we meet, to provide the grist for our creative mills.

Near the end of Spofford Alley a flight of red steps led us to a high red door which which was opened by a Chinese servant in red silk. You see a lot of red in Chinatown. It's symbolic—the color of happiness and vitality. Brides wear it instead of white (the Chinese color of mourning) and happy messages are always printed on red paper. Green represents the varied forms of life, while blue is for tranquility. Wealth and power are represented by yellow. All part of the Chinese belief system and the special world of Chinatown.

"I'm Hammett," I said. "We're here to see your master, Ching Hoo Lun." I'd notified Lun of our visit.

"Please follow," said the guy in red silk.

As we were ushered down a long, silent hallway toward the Great One's personal living quarters Erle whispered: "What if Lun clams up on us?"

I chuckled. "Not a chance. Not him. He talks like a river in flood. He'll tell us everything he knows."

"And you trust him?"

"Absolutely. He owes me."

"For what?"

"Never mind. I'll tell you all about it sometime."

Erle nodded as we reached a wide golden door at the end of the hallway. It was guarded by two jade dragons who looked like they'd enjoy making a meal of us.

"Please wait," said the servant, tapping lightly at the door. He nodded at a murmur from within. Meaning it was okay to enter.

We stepped into a familiar setting. I'd been here before a decade ago and the room looked just the same: partially draped wooden panels along the walls decorated with Chinese land-scapes in gold paint, several heavy black enameled chairs flanked by carved black teak tables, a couple of oil lamps, and a tasseled bronze gong in the far corner with a padded stick hanging next to it—to drive away demons. Chinese demons hate loud noise.

Maybe the room hadn't changed, but Ching Hoo Lun cer-tainly had. For one thing, he'd put on a lot of weight; Lun was now as fat as a temple Buddha and his double chin was now triple. He'd grown a beard of sorts which was little more than a mist of white along his cheeks. His gold fillings flashed at me as he bowed, smiling broadly.

"Ah, welcome!" he said, speaking with the hypnotic intensity of a roadshow tent preacher. "Ching Hoo Lun is greatly honored by this auspicious visit from his most valued friend, the re-nowned and redoubtable King of Crook-catchers."

He was sitting in some kind of high-backed ceremonial chair and didn't get up. As heavy as he was, maybe he *couldn't* get up. As I walked over to him he extended a thick-fingered hand. I shook it, giving him a little bow of my own.

"The wise and mighty Ching Hoo Lun should understand that I am a writer now, and no longer a detective," I said. Then I introduced Erle and there was more florid language from Lun as he waved each of us to a chair.

He wore a long sable-lined robe in stitched gold, gold satin trousers, and elaborate gold slippers studded with precious stones. Smallpox had run a devastating course through China-town when Lun was growing up and his skin was pitted and pock-marked. He peered at us through small round steel-rimmed spectacles, his eyes all-knowing. Just before I dropped out of school in Baltimore, when I was fourteen, I'd had a teacher with eyes like his.

Lun nodded toward a small red table at his left side. It was set with a delicate porcelain tea service and his man in red silk appeared to pour each of us a cup.

"Please to accept my humble offering," said Lun, as Red Silk filled our cups with steaming black tea. "This is a special blend of Oolong, which comes to us from the mountains of western Fujian province. You will note that the aroma is that of ripe peaches. It is my personal choice among a variety of splendid teas, reflecting the high esteem I hold for those who would choose to grace my simple abode with their illustrious presence."

It was quite a speech and I had to keep my head lowered over the cup to keep from grinning. The old boy certainly had a way with words.

We sipped the strong black brew and listened to him tell us, in high-flown phrases, about the origins of tea in ancient China, and how drinking it aids digestion and helps prevent tooth decay.

Finally I was able to tackle the subject we'd come to discuss; you have to plow through a lot of polite rhetoric to get down to basics when you talk to a Chinese.

"We are attempting to locate a particular gentleman, newly-arrived in Chinatown," I said. "His name is Wu Sing and it is our belief that he fled here from his home in Los Angeles."

Lun's triple chins quivered. "Fled? Was the gentleman of which you speak pursued here by enemies?"

"We don't think he was followed," I said. "But he felt he had to flee from his employer in order to preserve his life. Since your great wisdom is the envy of all Chinatown, we have come here to seek your generous and gracious aid in finding Wu Sing."

Lun nodded, pushing at his glasses. "It would be most improper of me to ask further questions—such as your reasons for wishing to locate this harried individual. Nor should I be obliged to inquire as to what, in precise terms, caused him to flee his home to come here. The answers are not of my concern and therefore shall not be solicited."

I nodded. What do you say to something like that? He was obviously damn curious, but didn't want to risk offending us with any personal questions.

"I am deeply shamed to inform you that I do not myself possess knowledge of this frightened gentleman, but if you will kindly allow me, I can perhaps direct you to a place wherein such information may presently reside."

"We would be most appreciative," Erle told him.

Lun peered uncertainly over the rim of his round spectacles at Erle. "Are you also a former Crook-catcher?"

"No, I'm a former lawyer," said Erle. "Now I'm a writer and I do books *about* lawyers."

"We have our own laws in Chinatown," said Lun darkly. He turned to face me. "You know Waverly Place?"

"Of course," I said.

"Then go there—to the Tien Hau Temple. Ask for a gentleman named Tu Fong. Among other activities, he is a caretaker at that establishment. Tu Fong is a most enterprising individual with. . ." Lun hesitated, searching for the proper phrase. "How do you say it? . . . with his extremities lodged inside many pastries."

I knew what he meant. "You're telling us he has his fingers in a lot of pies."

"Exactly so. Fong is indeed a man of many pies. It is quite likely that he will have some direct knowledge regarding the recent entry of He Who Flees."

"If you say so, I'm sure he will."

"Unfortunately, Tu Fong does not speak English. Only Mandarin and Cantonese."

"No problem," I assured Lun. I nodded toward Erle. "My friend here is fluent in Cantonese."

"Then," said Lun, "have your friend tell him that when the lotus is in bloom the soul stirs in joy."

I raised an eyebrow.

"The words will serve to identify you. Tu Fong will respond favorably."

"I'll remember," I said.

Lun smiled in another flash of gold. "I trust, in the happy future, upon your next visit to my humble quarters that you will allow this most unworthy one to offer you a specially prepared bowl of bird's nest soup and a serving of my personal blend of mu shu pork containing a healthy portion of black fungus which renders the blood fluid."

"Sounds delicious," I said. "Next time for sure."

We stood up.

"It is hoped that this lowly personage has perhaps been of some small service to his most worthy and revered friend, the Father of Detectives."

I bowed to him, unloaded more florid stuff about abiding friendship and eternal gratitude, and cut out with Erle for Waverly Place.

The fat man had given us a hot lead and I didn't want it to cool down.

TEN

According to Chinese folklore, Tien Hau is the goddess of heaven and sea. She's supposed to watch over and protect travelers, sailors, and prostitutes which, in Chinatown alone, must keep her plenty busy.

The Temple of Tien Hau, at 125 Waverly Place, is the oldest Chinese temple in the U.S., rising an impressive four stories from the street.

Once inside, we had no trouble locating Fong, a nervous little Cantonese with the pinpoint pupils of a heroin addict. With his finger in so many pies, I guess he didn't have any trouble supporting the habit.

I turned to Erle. "Tell him that when the lotus is in bloom the soul stirs in joy."

Erle passed this along.

Fong looked startled at the words, but immediately bowed us into his "personal chamber" at the rear section of the temple. The room was small and spotlessly maintained, with silk hangings of green, blue, and silver behind a long red couch. We all sat down on the couch.

Fong jabbered something at us, and Erle jabbered back. The only words I recognized were "Ching Hoo Lun."

I looked at Gardner. "What was that about?"

"Says he's deeply honored to be in the presence of the two illustrious friends of Ching Hoo Lun, and what can he do, miserable creature that he is, to serve our needs?"

"Get him to the point," I said. "Ask about Wu Sing. Say we need to find Sing chop chop."

More cross jabber from Erle and Fong. Then Gardner turned to me, grinning broadly. "We're in luck! Says he knows where Sing is."

"Great," I said. "Ask him for the address."

Erle did that. "A herbal shop on Jackson, near the end of Ross Alley. Wu Sing is staying in an apartment above the shop."

"Okay," I nodded, standing up from the couch. "Give him the routine about his having earned our eternal gratitude and let's get cracking."

Erle did that, too, and we headed for Jackson Street.

It was a short walk. I must have had a sour expression on my face because Gardner asked me what was wrong.

"What's wrong is that everything's so damn *right*."

"I don't get it."

I stopped walking to face him. "We come up here and talk to a couple of locals and, bingo!, we hit paydirt."

"Isn't that what we wanted?"

"It's all too easy," I said. "Too smooth and quick. Makes me nervous."

Erle gave me the old saw about not looking a gift horse in the mouth and what did I want to do anyway, comb through the whole length of Chinatown for a month trying to find Wu Sing?

"I'm just glad we made the right contacts," he said. Then he grinned at me. "Cheer up, Hammett. All we've got ahead of us is success."

And he seemed to be right. When we reached the herbal shop they'd had word of our coming.

"They," in this case, refers to the Yan family—father, mother, two big strapping sons, and a knockout daughter. They all met us at the door in a ring of smiles.

"Welcome to the humble shop of Feng Yan," said the father, who looked as if he'd been carved out of ancient ivory.

I said I was glad he knew English.

"My family, we are all most educated in speaking your language," he told me proudly. "Please enter."

Yan's shop was typical, permeated with the strong aroma of roots, berries, nuts, exotic flowers, seeds, and dates. Along each wall were countless rows of wooden drawers, each marked with Chinese characters to identify its herbal contents. A long glass display counter faced the entrance doors, topped by a hand-balance scale for weighing out the proper dosages.

Herbal shops are indigenous to Chinatown, dating back to a period when the Chinese immigrants had to depend solely on themselves for medical care. Most of the early Chinese settlers to the states brought along their own bags of herbal remedies. They didn't trust Western doctors and that hasn't changed much. The Chinese are certain their culture is superior to that of the "ghosts," as they call us Occidentals, and they're reluctant to depend on ghost doctors for their medical needs.

When Yan's daughter followed us into the shop I was struck by her slim beauty. Her black-lacquer hair was held in place by three jade butterflies; she wore gold earrings and a lavender jacket glittering with white stones, trousers of the same color, and soft traditional slippers. She was a real stunner, maybe twenty or so, with dark lustrous eyes.

"Wu Sing," I finally managed to say to the old man. "We came to see him. We were told he lives upstairs."

"What you have been told is true," said Feng Yan. "My sons will take you to Wu Sing." And he bowed us toward an inside stairway.

We were at the upper landing, at the top of the stairs, when they came at us. The two big Yan brothers. I was totally unprepared for an attack. The taller one slammed me to the floor and, before I could resist, clamped an arm around my neck in a classic stranglehold. It felt like a steel band. Dimly, as I began to black out from the pressure, I saw Erle go down across from me, the second Yan brother closing on him with a knife.

That's when a voice rang out: "Stop! Release them at once!"

The pressure on my neck vanished and I sat up choking for breath. Erle was pale and shaking. The two Yan brothers were facing a small, intense figure in an open doorway. He was dressed in a blue cotton shirt, cotton trousers, and straw sandals. I knew he had to be Wu Sing.

"This one," said the taller brother in a hard tone, gesturing toward me, "is a *detective* who has come to arrest you. He will take you back to Los Angeles where you will be tried for murder."

"He is not a detective," said Wu Sing. "I know this man. I have seen his photograph in the newspaper. He is a writer. And I do not fear writers."

By this time, the old man had joined us at the landing. He looked confused. "But . . . if Mr. Hammett is *not* a threat to us . . . why then did the honorable Ching Hoo Lun telephone to advise us of Mr. Hammett's true intent here in Chinatown?"

Before Sing could answer that one, Erle spun on me: "So *that's* what all the stuff about the 'blooming lotus' really meant! We were being set up."

"I *told* Lun I was no longer a detective," I said.

Sing took up the conversation. "Obviously, the illustrious Ching Hoo Lun did not believe that you were telling him the truth. He was afraid that you would take me away from my intended bride, Lulu Yan, to whom he is related by blood."

Lulu Yan was now with us, standing beside Wu Sing, and she verified his words. "I am the niece of Ching Hoo Lun. Uncle Lun knows that I am soon to marry Wu Sing. We have his most valued blessing."

That explained Lun's action. He was standing up for a member of his family—and family always comes first. He'd done a terrific job in pretending to know nothing about Sing or about what had happened back in L.A. on the *Lady*. But Sing had obviously filled him in, so Lun figured we were there to frame Wu Sing for the murders. A Chinese patsy to placate the cops. It was all a royal mix-up.

"We came here," I told Sing, "because we believed you were running from Bill Kelly."

"Why would I do such a thing?"

Erle replied. "Because you were aboard the *Lady* with your boss and you saw him gun down Tony Richetti and Clare Vanikis. You were a witness to the killings."

Sing shook his head slowly. "It is true that I was with my former employer on the night in question, but I witnessed nothing."

"But you were *there!*" I protested.

"Not at the time of the shooting," declared Wu Sing. "I accompanied Mr. Kelly on board and when he had no further need of my services I left the ship and returned to shore on the motor launch."

"Then if you didn't see anything, why did you quit Kelly the next day?" Erle asked him.

"I was tired of working for the ghosts," he said. "I wanted to be with my own people again and, although most of my relatives are in Los Angeles, my parents are here in Chinatown. They have approved of my forthcoming marriage."

The old man and his two sons did a great deal of bowing and apologizing before we left. How could they possibly earn our forgiveness for their grievous error? Perhaps, in atonement, they should each sacrifice a toe or a finger. I hoped they were kidding.

I told them it was all an innocent misunderstanding and that they should definitely keep all of their toes and fingers. Then I turned to Wu Sing. "We wish you and your intended bride great joy and prosperity and many sons." I checked my watch. "But now, if you'll excuse us, we have a train to catch."

And we got out of Chinatown. Fast.

After the wild goose chase in Frisco we were right back to square one—with nothing substantial tying Bill Kelly to the ship murders.

We both decided to call it quits.

Erle went back to his latest Mason book and I set up a meeting with Bill Faulkner at Musso & Frank's restaurant in Hollywood. I needed to snare another script assignment and I hoped Bill could put me in touch with one of the town's few movers and shakers I really had any respect for, Howard Hawks. His films were tough, direct, and masculine—cinema with muscle. Hawks had directed *Scarface* along with several others I'd admired. He had my kind of perspective on life and I figured we'd get along.

Faulkner, who lived and worked on his books in Oxford, Mississippi—wonderful novels such as *The Sound and the Fury* and *As I Lay Dying*—had come out to California to script for Hawks in '32 because he was broke. As he often said, "My books don't sell worth a tinker's dam." But I didn't know him back in '32; I met him later when he was visiting New York where we had a lot of good long nights together talking and drinking. We argued a lot—mostly about literature, women, and politics.

I hadn't seen Bill for awhile. He'd been holed up in Oxford working on a new book. But when *The Hollywood Reporter* stated that he was out here for Fox, working with Hawks again, I put in a call to the studio, got his phone number, and set up a meeting.

When I arrived at Musso's, Bill was waiting for me in a side booth. He stood up to shake my hand, an intense little man, barely above five feet, with sad Southern eyes and a mustache going to gray. He was in a neatly pressed white shirt and tweeds and his ever present pipe was on the table. I never saw Bill without that pipe.

"How ya doin' Dash?" he said in his low-pitched drawl, giving me a faint smile. Faulkner wasn't big on emotion. I slipped into the booth and we made some small talk about how much he missed his hominy grits in the morning and how he always wrote best in a rocking chair and how the studio couldn't seem to find one for his office.

"You'd think, with all them thousands a' props they got there, that they could find me one lousy rockin' chair," he declared.

Then I asked him if he'd started the new picture yet with Hawks. He shook his head.

"We're still in the talkin' stage," he told me. "But I know it's gonna be about trench warfare and that he's callin' it *Wooden Crosses*."

"Another war job, eh?"

"Yeah, they got me down as some kind of big authority on the war when all I did was spend a few months with the RAF up in Canada. As a raw cadet. Shoot, Dash, I learned about trench warfare from *All Quiet on the Western Front*."

He dug a silver flask out of his coat pocket and offered it to me. "Good bourbon. Kind you cotton to." I said I was trying to stay off the booze.

"Now, that's downright depressin' to hear," he said, taking a long hit on the flask. "Next, you'll be tellin' me you're givin' up women."

I grinned. "No, I plan to stay active in that department."

His sad eyes grew sadder. "You know, Dash, this movie-writin' business is an awful thing for grown folks to be doin'. I plain dunno how you stand it."

"The money's good," I said.

"Oh, sure, sure. An' that's the sole and only damn reason I come back—to pay off some killin' bills so's I can return to workin' on my novel. I tellya, Dash, I'm a book-writin' man an' I sure as hell don't belong out here."

"Apparently Hawks doesn't agree with you. He likes what you write for him."

"I try to turn out an honest day's work, try to give the fella what he wants whether it makes any sense or not. And most a' the time it doesn't."

He told me he even hated the climate.

"It's all this damn California sunshine. Where's your seasons? Leaf falls off a tree up in some dang canyon an' they're tellin' you it's winter. Awful place. Just awful!"

"It's not so bad once you get used to it," I said.

"Guarantee you, I never will." He fired up his pipe, puffing out blue-gray clouds, and asked: "Know anythin' about the ship murders?"

"No," I said flatly. I didn't feel like getting into it with Faulkner.

"People killin' people. Happens all the time out here."

"Happens everywhere," I said. "Human nature."

I was happy when he changed the subject. "You ever get down to the shop?"

He meant the Stanley Rose Bookshop, a kind of literary hangout here in Hollywood. Rose caters to authors, reserving a special "writer's retreat" in the rear of his store.

"Haven't been there for awhile," I said. "But I hear he's brought in some slot machines for the back room."

I finally got to the point, asking him if he could arrange a meeting with Hawks.

"Heck, yes, but it won't gain you nothin' cause Howard's not gonna be doin' any other projects for the next six months or more. Likes to take on one thing at a time. Right now, I'm his boy, but. . ." And he gave me his faint smile, "If I get riled enough at this darned place to quit an' go back to Oxford I'll give you a call an' maybe you can step in."

"It's a deal," I said.

He looked at me for a long moment through a shallow drift of pipe smoke. "Don't for the life a' me know how you do it."

"Do what?"

"Stay sane out here. I've only been back a week an' I'm half-cuckoo already."

"I just roll with the punches," I told him.

"You workin' on a new book?"

"Trying to," I said. "Not much luck so far."

He grinned. After that we ordered some sand dabs and didn't say a whole lot while we ate. Then he said he had to leave for a story conference at Fox. "They need my trench expertise."

He got up, shook my hand again, and ambled out into the "damn California sunshine."

I felt a little sorry for him.

And a lot sorrier for myself.

Back in Pacific Palisades, I was building a tall strawberry soda to soothe my nerves when Ray Chandler showed, rolling up to the house in his big cream-colored Duesenberg. Buddy met him at the door and brought him down to the rumpus room.

"Hello, Raymond," I said. "Care to join me in a double-dip?"

"No, thanks," he said. "But I wouldn't mind some black coffee, so long as it's fresh."

Buddy brought him some.

"Erle told me about your recent excursion to San Francisco," Chandler said. "Frustrating."

"That's the word for it."

Ray took a stool at the ice cream bar and put his cup on the counter. "As I understand it, you promised Shaw you'd nail Big Bill Kelly for him."

"Then you understand it wrong. He asked me to go after Kelly, but I said nix, that I was out of it."

"Then why did you go to Chinatown?"

"Because Erle came to me with what both of us thought was a real hot lead on putting Kelly away." I shrugged. "It fizzled."

"So now you're out of it?"

"Yep," I said. "What I'm trying to do at the moment is hook another screen job."

"Any luck?"

"Not so far. Leland is looking around for me. When I do connect again I've promised myself that I will refrain from calling the producer a pinhead. I'll eat my humble pie."

"I can't see you as an arse-kisser."

"I don't have to kiss anybody's ass. All I have to do is keep my mouth shut. Bill Faulkner's got the right idea about working in this burg: Give them what they want even if it doesn't make any sense."

"I haven't talked to Shaw, but Erle says—"

"Never mind what Erle says," I cut in. "The sooner we can all forget what happened on the *Lady* the better. The Cat's Eye is gone and Kelly is out of our reach."

"Well, not exactly. I came here today to tell you I can arrange a meeting with him."

"Hell, if I wanted to meet with Kelly, which I don't, I'd just take a run out to his ship."

"It's not that easy. The word is he's not in circulation anymore, that he's not seeing anybody. Been keeping to his cabin on *The Lucky Horseshoe*. You wouldn't be able to talk to him."

"Fine. We have nothing to talk about."

"He killed Tony and the girl to get the jeweled skull. There's a *lot* to talk about."

"And what good would it do?"

"I'd just like to see his face when we tell him about finding his lighter at the murder scene."

"He'll give us the horse laugh. You've been reading too many of your own stories, Ray. Guys like Kelly are *rocks*. They don't budge, don't admit anything. If we caught Bill Kelly with a bloody knife in his hand and a dead man on the floor at his feet he'd swear he was framed. So why see him?"

"But you *will* go with me if I can set up a meeting?"

"Why should I?"

"Because I'd feel a lot better if you were along."

"I still don't see what you expect to gain by this."

Chandler finished his coffee and got off the stool to stand in front of me. "Maybe nothing. But I want to hear what Kelly has to say about the lighter." He gave me a long hard stare. "Can I count on you, Dash?"

I shrugged again. "In addition to this being a total waste of time, it *could* be dangerous. I've already been thrown into the ocean once. I don't fancy the idea of having it happen again."

"We'll tell Kelly we've left word with people that we're seeing him. That way, he won't try anything."

"It's stupid and it's risky."

"Humor me."

"Damn you, Chandler," I said.

He was grinning.

ELEVEN

The following night Ray had set things up with Bill Kelly's people and they provided a speedboat to take us out to the *Horseshoe*. We were met at the pier in Santa Monica by one of Kelly's hoods, a thin-faced, slit-eyed character with all the warmth of a swamp alligator. He didn't say anything as he handed us into the boat, which was long, low and powerful. A gold horseshoe was painted on her bow.

A brisk ocean wind made the sea dance under us and the small boat bucked through the choppy water like a Coney Island roller coaster. Kelly's gambling ship was slightly larger than the *Lady* and the ocean swells didn't affect her much. Coming in, we could hear a band playing "Everything is Hotsy Totsy Now," which made me think of Scott Fitzgerald. I had a sudden flash of concern for him. Somehow, Scotty seemed lost and out of place here in the 1930s, as if his true self, his essence, lay buried back in the Jazz Age, like a fly trapped in amber. He reminded me of Dick Diver, Scotty's tragic hero in his novel *Tender is the Night*; Fitzgerald seemed inexorably linked to darkness and despair.

On board the *Horseshoe* a large crowd flowed around us, chattering like magpies, their eyes hot and fevered with visions of future wins at table and wheel. With Richetti dead, and with the *Lady* still undergoing fire-damage repair, Kelly had the ocean all to himself. Although this was a Monday night, generally the slowest of the week, Big Bill was reaping a rich harvest.

I felt a strong urge to try my hand at faro, but we weren't there to gamble, so I resisted the temptation.

Beyond the main salon, Kelly's alligator man led us to the lower-deck cabins. He hadn't said a word since we'd left the pier and he remained tight-lipped and silent. Even when we reached Kelly's personal quarters at the end of a long, thickly carpeted passageway, he still didn't speak, just raised a warning hand.

Facing us were double oak doors, varnished and gleaming. Our man used a key to open the first one, waved us through into a waiting area, then thoroughly patted us down for weapons. He seemed disappointed not to find any. Then he code-rapped on the inner door, which was opened by another of Kelly's unsmiling beefcakes.

We stepped inside to find Big Bill waiting for us, dressed in a monogrammed yellow-silk robe over yellow-silk pajamas. He stood up from a long, leather, metal-studded couch to shake hands with each of us. At six five, he lived up to his nickname; everything about him was big, including his smile.

"Welcome aboard, gents," he said. "These here—" and he gestured toward a group of four tough characters in the room, "are my personal bodyguards. They'll stay while we have our little chat."

All four of them stared at us sullenly; maybe they didn't like writers.

Kelly had a long, violent history behind him. A jagged white scar ran down the left side of his neck, to the jawline, the result of a knife fight as a young man in Detroit; he'd been fighting since he could walk. Owned his first gun when he was ten. At nineteen, he was part of a Detroit gang known as the "Stompers" because they stomped people—robbing their victims, often beating them. Old folks were special targets. When Prohibition came along, Kelly began hijacking trucks, got into smuggling, and eventually opened his own speakeasy, becoming the unofficial King of Bathtub Gin. Shot in a gang war, he spent six months in a Chicago hospital, after which he was tried for murder and got the charge dropped on a legal technicality.

When he bought his first gambling ship it was blown out of the water before he could open it for business; rumor pinned the dynamite job on Tony Richetti, who didn't appreciate competition. After Kelly opened *The Lucky Horseshoe*, in 1930, the two became locked in a bitter feud, with more or less even results until the night Richetti was gunned down. Big Bill Kelly, who had made many friends in high places due to freely distributed cash payouts, was now the undisputed champ, the Al Capone of the Pacific.

I didn't know much about his personal life beyond the fact that he was divorced and had a teenage daughter. Of course I'd heard about his string of women, but you expect that from a gambling kingpin.

Kelly nodded toward the couch: "Take a load off. Drinks?" We said no thanks.

"Okay, then," he said, "let's get to it. I agreed to see you two because you're supposed to have something that belongs to me. Now I happen to be a curious kind of jasper, so—what is it?"

"This," I said, tossing the gold cigarette lighter to him. Big Bill caught it with his left hand, stared at it, then looked up, frowning. "Where'd you find my lighter?"

"In Tony's cabin," I said. "On the night he was put away."

Chandler was pissed off at me. "Dammit, Dash, I didn't know you were going to give it *back* to him. It's evidence!"

"Sure," I nodded. "Worthless evidence. No use hanging onto the thing."

112

"Your pal's right," Kelly grinned, slipping the lighter into the pocket of his robe. He was handed a Scotch by one of his flunkies and, sipping it, he eased back on the leather couch. "So you boys think I put away Richetti and the frail?"

"That's what we think," Ray said.

"Hey, lemme tell you, I shed no tears for old Tony. He was one mean-assed piece of goods. Not only did he blow up my first ship, but he tried to have me killed on at least three occasions. I got witnesses."

"So you did to him what he tried to do to you," I said.

"Should I confess?" He looked at his boys and began to laugh. All four of his flunkies laughed with him.

"I told Ray that coming here was a stupid idea," I said.

He swung toward Chandler. "Why did you come?"

"I wanted to look into the face of a man who could do what you've done. Call it 'creative research.' That's as good a term as any."

"Gonna put me in one of your stories?"

"Could be," said Chandler. "I like to be as realistic as possible."

"What if I told you I didn't pull off that ice job on the Lady?"

"We didn't expect you to admit it," I said.

"You were there that night," Ray said. "We know that for certain."

"Because you found my lighter?"

"That's one reason—but also because a man who worked for you, Wu Sing, told us he accompanied you to the ship."

"Okay," nodded Kelly. "So I was on board the Lady that night—but there are two things you better get straight."

I noticed he was holding his drink in his left hand, the same one he'd used to catch the lighter, and I suddenly realized why: to keep his right hand free for the automatic he undoubtedly had under his robe. Gunmen in the Old West used to do that, keep

113

their right hands free for action. Even with four armed body-guards in the same room, Kelly was ready to draw and fire at a split second's notice.

"So go ahead, tell us two things we should know," I said.

"Yeah," nodded Ray. "We're listening."

"One, I never lost my lighter aboard the *Lady*. And two, I left before the fire broke out and *before* the double gundown."

"You think we believe that?" asked Ray.

Kelly smiled, sipping his drink. "I don't give a rat's ass what you believe. Even if I told you I did the killings, admitted it outright, you couldn't do shit about it."

"True enough," I said.

"So there's no percentage in lying to you. I don't gain any-thing." Kelly gestured for another drink and a full Scotch glass replaced the empty one. Apparently, his bodyguards also filled in as servants; they didn't seem to mind. "Now, do you two want to hear the truth?"

"That would be peachy," said Chandler.

"Okay, then." Kelly relaxed again, savoring the fresh drink. "I gave up cigarettes a year ago, after I developed a bad cough, but I still like to carry the lighter with me for luck. Like a rabbit's foot. About a week before all hell broke out on the *Lady* I discovered that my lighter was missing. I'd been to the opera—you two ever go to the opera?"

Chandler and I shook our heads.

"You don't know what you're missing," declared Kelly. "Opera is great. Clears your soul the way a good dump clears your bowels."

"I never thought of it quite that way," I admitted.

"Me, I'm nuts about Puccini. *La Tosca* just knocks me cold. And *Madame Butterfly* is a real humdinger. Makes me cry like a baby."

I'd never have connected Kelly with opera. The thought of Big

Bill stuffed into a tuxedo and tearing up over Puccini was an image to ponder.

"Did you know the first public opera house was opened in Venice in 1637?"

"No," said Ray flatly. "I didn't know that."

"Anyhow, here I was at the opera, pushing through the lobby after the last act, being bumped around pretty good by the crowd—and that's when it happened."

"What happened?" I asked.

"I discovered my lucky lighter was missing. A dip was obviously working the lobby and he'd slipped his mitt into my new tux, smooth as a gopher down a hole, and filched the lighter. At first, I thought it was just the luck of the draw, that I was in the wrong place at the wrong time. Now that you guys tell me the lighter turned up on the *Lady* the night of the kill, I see it from a whole new angle."

"How do you mean?" Ray asked him.

"I mean that I'm now sure that Julie *ordered* the snatch so the lighter could be left in the cabin to frame me. Julie tried to set me up for the double knockover." He chuckled. "Only it didn't work, did it? Sure, you bozos found it, just like Julie planned, but you were smart enough to know the lawboys would laugh it off if you brought it to them as evidence. It wasn't enough to cinch the frame."

"So who's this Julie," I wanted to know. "Ex-girlfriend of yours? A woman scorned?"

"No woman. Julie is what I've always called Tony's son, Julio. Take my word for it, Julio Richetti's the gink who pulled off the ice job, not me."

"Why would he kill his own father?" Chandler asked.

"They never got along," said Kelly. "Tony used to beat the kid real regular when Julie was growing up. With a leather strap.

115

The kid hated Tony worse than poison. And when he finally got the chance, he put him away."

"Does he have any brothers or sisters?" I asked.

"Yeah, one sister, Ruthie. Ruth Anne. Year younger than him. Once she was grown, she refused to have anything to do with her father's gambling operation. To her, Daddy was a crook, a disgrace to the family."

"Does she get along with her brother?"

"They get along okay. But Julie and her were never close. At least, that's what I've been told."

"Why did he kill Clare Vanikis?" Ray asked.

Kelly shrugged. "Who knows? Maybe she just got in the way. I don't think he planned on it. It was Tony he was after."

If Kelly was telling us the truth then he didn't have the jeweled skull; Julio Richetti had it. From the way Kelly talked, he seemed totally unaware of the Cat's Eye and how it tied into the double killings. But maybe he was lying to hide the fact that he'd grabbed it.

I asked: "Why would Julio Richetti try to frame you?"

"The kid never liked me. We had a couple of incidents in the past where I hijacked some booze trucks of his. Course, that was before I bought the *Horseshoe*."

"Uh-huh," I said.

"Julie did me a big favor, knocking off his old man. The fact that he tried to frame me in the bargain doesn't change that. Business is terrific these days. I got no complaints."

"Where's Julio now?" asked Chandler.

"He took a powder," nodded Kelly. "Nobody knows where he is. Maybe when the *Lady*'s ready to go back into operation he'll show up again and pick up from where his old man left off."

"Do you have his sister's address?" I asked.

"Naw—but she lives somewhere in Long Beach. Or so I've heard. Works at a bank—a clerk or a teller, something like that."

When we stood up to leave Kelly walked us to the door. His bodyguards kept their eyes tight on us, like four hunting cats.

Kelly put a hand on Ray's shoulder. "When you write me into one of those stories of yours," he said, "you remember to send me a copy, okay?"

"Sure," nodded Ray. "I'll do that."

"I hope you two boys got a little better opinion of Big Bill Kelly after what all I told you."

"Yeah, we figure you're a real sweetheart," I said, and we left his cabin, taken back to the speedboat by our alligator-cold friend. On the return trip to the pier in Santa Monica he finally spoke to us. One sentence. Eight words.

"You two mugs are lucky to be alive."

I guess we were at that.

"Well, how do you rate what Kelly told us?"

Ray was driving me back to the Palisades in his Duesy when he asked me the question. I thought about it for a long moment before answering.

"He's a gutter rat and I think he's lying. Kelly admits he's damned glad that Tony is out of the picture. He had every reason to get rid of him, *especially* when he could waltz off with the Cat's Eye."

"He never mentioned it."

"He couldn't afford to—not if he expected us to believe the line he was handing out."

"Why should he lie?"

"Lying is as natural as breathing to scum like Kelly. He enjoyed playing with us, seeing how much we'd swallow."

"But don't you think somebody should follow up on Julio Richetti—just to cover that angle?"

"I'll check him out, but I don't expect to come up with anything. The whole Julio routine was designed to throw us off the track. All part of Kelly's effort to impress us with his innocence."

Ray shook his head, easing the Duesy around a slow-moving Helm's Bakery truck. A milky night fog had moved in from the ocean, damp and cold. "I still don't see why Big Bill Kelly should be trying to impress a couple of writers."

"Maybe because of what you told him."

"Huh?"

"About putting him in a story. To Kelly, that's like getting a page-one write-up in the papers. Appealed to his ego. He wants to look good in print."

"I don't know," Ray muttered. "I think he just might have been giving us the straight goods. Sometimes, Hammett, you're too damn cynical."

"When it comes to gutter rats, I'm always cynical," I said.

"But you *will* check on Julio and let me know what you find out?"

"I said I would."

When we arrived at my place in the Palisades I thanked Ray for the ride.

"Bet you're glad I talked you into meeting Kelly," he said.

"It was interesting," I admitted. "Like picking up a damp rock to see what's crawling around underneath. Had a certain fascination."

Ray put the car in gear. "Phone me when you get anything."

"*If* I get anything," I said.

And Ray drove off in the big convertible, a cream-colored ghost blending into the fog.

Daytime. High noon. A blazing sun above Wilshire Boulevard. I was watching a parade.

Big Bill Kelly was riding down Wilshire on the back of a tall pink elephant and all the people along the street were cheering, with several women hysterically screaming his name, waving their lace handkerchiefs at him.

Kelly smiled broadly, waving back. He was dressed like a cowboy, in fringed white buckskins with a big ten-gallon hat on his head. His boots were polished to a high gloss, set off with silver spurs, and he had a pearl-handled six-shooter strapped around his waist.

I was at the edge of the crowd as he passed and I turned to one of the screaming women. "What the hell's *wrong* with you, lady? This guy you're cheering for is a murdering bastard who belongs in the electric chair."

She hauled off and slapped me hard across the face. "I won't listen to this kind of talk about an innocent man like Bill Kelly," she said. There were tears in her eyes. "You have no right to say those awful things about him."

Before I could get off a reply Kelly stopped the elephant, slid to the ground, and walked over to me. He had his right hand on the butt of the six-gun.

"This bozo givin' you trouble, ma'am?" he asked the woman. She was young and striking, with a full figure and large doe eyes. She stared at Kelly with those big eyes, transfixed, then suddenly threw herself into his arms, kissing him with frantic passion.

He pushed her away and came right up to me, a snarl twisting his face. "You lay off me, Hammett. I don't put up with loose talk from punks."

I swung at him, connecting with a savage left hook. I followed up with a Sunday punch to the jaw that sent him crashing to the street. He twisted, clawing at the six-shooter.

I kicked the gun out of his hand, grabbed him by the front of his fancy buckskin shirt, and dragged him to his feet. The crowd around us was hissing and booing.

"You people are all saps," I yelled. "This rotten piece of putrefying dogmeat is—"

I stopped in mid-sentence. Under my grip, Kelly had turned into Joe Shaw.

He blinked at me. "Jeez, Dash, why are you treating me like this? Didn't I always pay you the top rate at *Black Mask*? Didn't I encourage you to extend your Continental Op stuff into book-length novels? Didn't I say nice things about you in my editorials?"

"Uh . . . sure, Joe, sure," I stammered, confused by the switch from Kelly to Shaw. "You were square with me all down the line."

"Then why did you quit writing for me?"

"You know the answer to that one. I needed money. Not pulp money, *Hollywood* money. Writing for you was a luxury I couldn't afford anymore."

"I kept you alive in the Twenties," he protested. "You were mighty glad to cash those story checks."

"That was different. I had a family to support and pulp writing was the only way to do it."

I stepped back, letting go of his shirt. He wiped a thread of blood from his mouth which had spattered down to stain his white buckskins. I looked at my knuckles; they were red and raw from hitting him. I felt like a louse.

"Look," Joe said. "My elephant is waiting and I gotta get back on board. But there's something I have to know."

"What is it?"

"Why can't you *believe* what people tell you? What makes you so goddamn cynical?"

"Maybe I spent too many years on the street with Pinkerton," I said. "Had to deal with too many lowlife yeggs, with dopers and gunmen and crooked dames. You grow a hard shell over your soul for self-protection. If you're not hard-souled, you don't survive."

"Do you believe me when I tell you I didn't kill Tony and Clare?" Shaw asked.

"Yes. Yes, I do."

"Well, then, for Christ's sake, get off my ass!" shouted Bill Kelly (Joe was gone), climbing back on his elephant.

I watched the big pink beast shamble on down Wilshire while the crowd cheered.

TWELVE

The dream about Kelly meant something. It was a message from my subconscious telling me that I *was* becoming too damn cynical—and that maybe Bill Kelly had told the truth about Julio being the trigger man. Therefore, the next step was logical: contact Ruth Anne Richetti and try to locate her brother.

Of course, by now, I'd been pitched right back into the case—and I knew that if Julio Richetti was indeed responsible for the killings I was asking for trouble in attempting to run him to ground. But that trip out to the *Horseshoe* had set me in motion again so I said what the hell and looked up Ruthie in the Long Beach phone book.

Sure enough, there she was: R.A. Richetti. Ruth Anne herself. It was Sunday; she'd be home, not at work. I dialed her number and she answered on the second ring.

"My name is Peter Collinson," I said, "and I need to see you as soon as possible."

If Julio was on the run his trail was already cold, but I figured there was no use letting it get any colder.

"Is this some kind of sales gimmick?" Her voice was suspicious and unfriendly.

"Oh, no, nothing like that. I just need to see you."

"About what?"

"It's personal. Something I can't discuss over the phone. Could I come over this afternoon? To your place—or maybe you might prefer to meet in a restaurant somewhere?"

"Why should I talk to you? Who are you? Your name doesn't ring any bells."

I didn't want her to know my real name, not at this stage at least. She might have read about me and connect me to Tony. I'd used "Collinson" as the byline for some of my early stuff in *Mask*. In fact, the pen name was on my first Continental Op yarn. In gang lingo it means "nobody's son."

"This is about your brother," I told her. "He's in trouble."

"That's not exactly hot news. Julio is usually in some kind of trouble."

"This is bad. He said I should talk to you."

"Are you a friend of his?"

I played a long shot: "We went to grade school together."

If she'd asked "What school?" I'd have been stuck for an answer, but it seemed the right thing to say—and it worked.

She agreed to see me, giving me specific directions on how to reach her apartment in Long Beach. "I'll be outside by the pond," she told me, "feeding the fish. And I'll be wearing a big cartwheel hat with sunflowers on it."

I had Buddy take me there.

"When am I going to get paid, Chief?" he asked me as we cleared the suburbs of L.A. and headed south.

"As soon as I hook another picture," I told him. "Leland is nosing around for me. I'm sure he'll turn up something."

Buddy grunted. "So you're flat, eh?"

"Only on a temporary basis," I said. "As you know, my potential is unlimited. Just a matter of time before I get another assignment."

He sighed, keeping his eyes on the road. The limo purred along like a big kitten. Buddy was a crack mechanic and he kept the car in tiptop shape. Now he flicked a glance at me through the rearview mirror.

"Sometimes I ask myself—why do I work for a writer? Nobody in his right mind should work for a writer."

"Hey, things aren't so bad. Our rent's paid for the next two months. At least you've got a roof over your head. Considering we're in a national depression, you're lucky to be working at all."

"So what are we going to eat? Double-dip strawberry sodas?"

"We'll never starve," I assured him. "You like turkey, don't you?"

"Sure, I like turkey."

"Then—no problem. I'll just go up to Turkey Hill and grab one of Ben Hecht's birds."

Buddy shook his head. He was flicking the limo through traffic with the ease of a racing driver. We were on the coast road and I could smell the ocean. The air was clear as scrubbed glass.

"Just trust me, kid," I said to him. "I'll be on another picture before you can say Jack Robinson. Feel it in my bones."

"Right now I'm feeling it in my wallet."

We passed the LONG BEACH CITY LIMITS sign at the side of the road.

"Will you trust me?" I asked.

"Sure. What *else* can I do?"

I've always liked Long Beach. The grand old wooden hotels with their manicured green lawns remind me of the South. There's a tranquil, lazy kind of grace here; the Hollywood hustle and bustle seems a long way off, something that's part of another world.

Ruth Richetti's apartment building was one of the newer

brick-and-stone jobs with a wide inner courtyard set off by a sizable goldfish pond. That's where Ruthie was, scattering bits of fish food into the water, the big straw hat on her head. When she looked up I saw that her eyes were deep, dark violet, almost a royal purple. She gave me a long, slow, searching look. "So you're Collinson."

I said I was.

"Let's go inside where we can talk."

I looked around. The courtyard was deserted.

"What's wrong with where we are?" I asked. "Nobody's around to hear us if that's what worries you."

"I don't give a damn what people hear or don't hear. What I need is a drink, and the drinks are inside." She leveled her violet eyes on me. "You look like you could use one."

"I never drink in the afternoon," I said. Then I grinned. "At least not for the past six months."

"Got a booze problem, eh?"

"I'm handling it."

We walked across the edge of the grassed patio into her ground-floor apartment. Newspapers were stacked everywhere. On chairs, tables, on the sofa, and on the floor along each wall.

"You'll have to pardon the mess," she said, clearing a space for me to sit on one of the chairs. "I've got a thing for newspapers. I keep thinking I'll want to read the articles again, so I hang on to every paper I get. Crazy, huh?"

"Eccentric might be a better word for it, Miss Richetti. You don't strike me as the crazy type."

"Thanks for the vote of confidence."

She poured a healthy slug of gin into a tumbler, added some quinine water, and put a wedge of lime in it. "Gin and tonic," she said. "The latest thing. Sure you don't want one?"

"I'm sure."

She kicked aside a bundle of papers and settled on the edge of the flowered sofa. Her eyes were locked on me again. "You never went to grade school with my brother and your name isn't Collinson."

"What makes you say that?"

"Well, for one thing, Daddy had private tutors for Julio and me when we were kids; we never attended an outside elementary school. Later, we both went to Hampstead Academy, which is an exclusive boarding school for the offspring of rich-but-socially-unacceptable parents—like gamblers. Since you lied about the school, my guess is you're probably lying about your name. Am I wrong?"

"You're a very sharp young woman," I said, meaning it. "If you knew I wasn't telling you the truth over the phone, then why did you agree to see me?"

"Ever own a cat?"

"No," I said.

"Cats are curious about everything. I'm that way—like a cat."

"You have cat's eyes," I observed.

"Got them from my mother. Hers were deep, dark violet, just like mine." She squeezed the lime wedge into her drink and took a sip. "Now, how about starting all over. Just who are you and what's your real name?"

"I'm a screen writer—when I can find a job, that is—and my name's Hammett. I've done a few books."

"I've read about you," she said, nodding.

"In the papers, naturally."

"Naturally." She smiled. "I've seen your picture there, too. I *knew* you looked familiar. M-G-M is doing your *Thin Man* movies, right?"

"Yeah. They've got a new one on the stove."

"What's it like for you, being famous?"

I shrugged. "Hemingway is famous. I just wrote a few detective stories, got 'em printed, and the next thing I know I'm in Hollywood, hacking out silly scripts."

"My father was famous," she said darkly. "For all the wrong reasons."

I didn't say anything to that. She sipped at the gin and tonic, looking down at her hands. "He was an evil man. Corrupt and evil. I'm not sorry he's dead."

"Then you didn't love him?"

"Love him!" She raised her head, eyes fierce. "I *hated* him! Since I was old enough to know good from evil I hated Tony Richetti." She spat out his name as a priest might spit out Satan's.

"I understand your brother felt the same way."

"He hated Daddy as much as I did, but there was a difference. Julio *needed* him. He lived off Daddy's gambling money. That's why I have such contempt for him. He's been a leech—a weak, money-sucking leech."

"Did he hate your father enough to kill him?"

She stared at me with those deep violet eyes. A muscle twitched along her jaw. "Is that the trouble you mentioned on the phone? Is Julio being charged with Daddy's murder?"

"No, not yet," I said. "But he ran out right after the shooting, and I'd like to find out why."

"What's a movie writer doing chasing down murderers?"

"I've been asking myself the same question." I sighed. "Has something to do with paying off a debt to an old friend I once worked for. But I'll skip the reasons, if you don't mind. The point is, I need to find your brother and I came here to ask you where he might be right now."

She shook her head. "We don't stay in touch anymore," she said. "He knows how disgusted I was with him—the way he sucked around Daddy. I never tried to hide my feelings. Anyway—I haven't seen my brother for several months so I don't think I can help you find him."

"Have you talked to Julio since the shooting?"

"No, not a word."

127

"Is he maybe living with a woman?"

She snorted. "Julio's *always* with a woman. Females are like candy to him and he has a real sweet tooth. But I wouldn't know who he's with now. And I don't care."

"You have his last address?"

"He was renting a beach house in Malibu. I called there after Daddy's death but the phone had been disconnected. I drove over and the owner told me Julio had left abruptly, with no forwarding address. So when he didn't show up for Daddy's funeral, I wasn't surprised."

"And you have no idea where he might be now?"

"No idea."

"Yet you used the word 'think.' You said: 'I don't *think* I can help you find him.' Why did you qualify your answer?"

She smiled at this. "You have a very sharp ear, Mr. Hammett."

"Part of my business. All writers need to know how to listen." I didn't tell her I mastered the art when I was with Pinkerton; no use getting into any of that. "Well, what about it, *can* you help me find him?"

"Maybe," she said. "At least I can give you the name of a man he used to hunt with. They called themselves fellow 'sportsmen,' if you consider it sport to kill a helpless animal with a high-powered rifle."

"Who is this hunter?"

"His name is Jeffry Chester."

"Where can I find him?"

"He does radio. A local actor. Usually works out of KFI on Hope Street. You know the station?"

"I've heard of it."

"It's at Tenth and Hope. They do a lot of shows there. Last I heard he was one of their regulars. Filling in various character roles. I remember he had a running part in one of their daytime serials. Chester might know where Julio is. They were real buddy-buddy for awhile."

I stood up to take her hand. It was cool and slender. "You've been a great help and I really appreciate it. I also appreciate your honesty. Sorry I had to start things off by lying to you."

"That's okay. You had no way of knowing whether or not I'd cooperate. And maybe if you'd told me who you really were, I wouldn't have."

She pushed at her dark hair, her eyes sad and reflective. "I hope you find Julio. He *could* have killed Daddy. If he had a strong enough reason."

I thought of the Cat's Eye. "Maybe he did."

"Good-bye, Mr. Hammett," she said, giving me her hand again.

She looked very sensual, standing there with her lips full and moist, those violet eyes, and that dark mass of hair framing her tanned face. At another time, under other conditions, I might have made a play for her.

As it was, I just nodded and walked back outside to Buddy, who had the limo door open for me.

"Tenth and Hope," I said.

He didn't ask me any questions on the way to KFI so I didn't have to give him any answers.

I felt like a detective again.

Which was crummy.

THIRTEEN

I left Buddy with the limo in a public parking lot and walked to the corner of Tenth and Hope. I wasn't sure I had the right building since the entire lower floor was occupied by an automobile showroom—part of the Earle C. Anthony Packard dealership. A gangly, tow-haired kid on roller skates was standing by the entrance. He blinked at me through round glasses.

"Is this the KFI building?" I asked him.

"Sure is!" he declared. His voice was high-pitched and full of energy. "I just got Jack Benny." He nodded, pointing at the doors. "Mr. Benny came right through there. And last week I got Orson Welles."

"You talking autographs?"

"Sure am!" He patted a thick leather book sticking out of a rear pocket. "Got dozens and dozens. It's one of the best collections in the whole city! Even got W.C. Fields when I skated over to M-G-M, and he's a tough one. Usually they're in a hurry, the stars, and they just sign their name fast, but sometimes they inscribe 'To Ray.' Those are the best ones."

I was amused by the kid's enthusiasm. "Is Ray your first or last name?"

"First," he said. "It's Ray Douglas Bradbury, and someday people will know who I am. I'm going to be a famous writer like Edgar Rice Burroughs, with my name on lots of books!"

"Ever sold anything?"

"Heck no, but I'm only fifteen," he declared. "It's just a matter of time, though. I write every day."

"Between roller skating sessions?"

"I do this afternoons. Mornings, I write. Before school, of course. Got my own typewriter. What do you do?"

"I'm a detective."

"Wow!" said young Bradbury. "You here to arrest somebody?"

"Could be," I said.

"Wow!" His eyes were popping behind the glasses. "Are you carrying a gun?"

"Not at the moment."

"But you own one?"

"Don't all detectives own guns?"

He grinned. "Hey, you're pullin' my leg."

"Maybe a little," I admitted. "Look, I have to see a man at KFI. Where's the studio?"

"Third floor," Bradbury said. "You go through the showroom and take the elevator up."

"I'm obliged, Ray," I told him. "Good luck with your writing career."

"Thanks," the energized boy said. "And good luck with your criminal case!"

I nodded, entered the building, and was halfway to the elevator when a salesman hailed me.

"Hi! I'm Al Bright!"

You sure are, I thought. Bright as a brass button and chipper as a squirrel. Par for the course in car salesmen.

"What do you think of our brand new '36 models?" he asked.

I looked at the shiny display cars spread out along the big showroom floor. Six Packards. In a variety of colors, from black to yellow—and all with whitewalls. They looked good and I said so.

"We just got these shipped in to us this week," he told me, showing a lot of teeth. "They're our new one-twenty models— spanking fresh off the assembly line."

"Nice," I said.

"You know, sir, for a super quality car like the Packard you're naturally going to have to pay more, but you can drive away one of these beauties for just under a thousand. Sure, that's a lot of money for an automobile, but look what you're getting. Even the whitewalls are standard."

"Nice," I said again.

"Golly, you'd have to pay almost that much for the new Nash Ambassador—and there's just no comparison. Not with a Packard." He gave me another toothy smile. "Just ask the man who owns one. That's our slogan!"

"Uh-huh," I said. "I've heard it before."

"I assume you're in the market for a great new automobile?"

"I don't drive," I said flatly. "So I'm not in the market."

The salesman kept smiling. "You will be someday. When you're ready to buy, come back and see me." He walked briskly away, his reflection dancing along the polished side of a new 120, and then he was gone. Customer hunting in the midst of the Depression. Silently, I wished him luck.

Inside the creaking elevator cage, heading for the third floor, I thought about how surprised Joe Shaw would be at my present involvement in the Cat's Eye caper. Good title for a *Black Mask* yarn. Maybe Gardner could use it for one of his Jenkins novelettes. Then again, maybe not. Let him think up his own titles.

When I stepped from the elevator a hard-looking blonde in a green knit dress, sitting behind the reception desk, looked me up and down and asked my business.

"I've been told that an actor named Jeffry Chester works for KFI. Is he here today?"

"He's inside." She jerked a thumb toward a back door along the wall with a blinking red bulb above it. "Doing a show. But I can't let you in. I can't let anybody in during a show."

"I won't disturb him. I just want to—"

"Hey, forget it!" she snapped. "I wouldn't let Eleanor Roosevelt in during a show. You read me, mister?"

I frowned, knowing that nothing I said would get me past her. "I'd better talk to the station manager."

"That would be Mr. Freberg. But he's not in the building. Maybe I could let you talk to the assistant manager."

"I'd appreciate that," I said.

Giving me another hard lookover, she pressed a button on her desk and a young fellow in his mid-twenties stepped out of a hallway to my left. He was neatly dressed and looked convivial.

"I'm Norman Corwin," he said. "Is there some kind of problem?"

I decided that I needed to warm up Norman before trying to talk my way into the studio. I'd gotten nowhere fast with the blonde. "There's no problem," I assured him. "But could we possibly sit down for a minute?"

"Of course." He nodded toward a long leather couch and we settled into it. "Now, what can I do for you?"

"Mind if I ask a personal question?"

He looked a bit startled. "That depends on the question. Just what is it you want to know?"

"I'm very interested in this profession, how one breaks into the radio business and all, but I'm just starting to learn about it. I really don't know that much. I'd like to find out how *you* got started. Mind telling me?"

"Do you mean you want to manage a station?"

"Oh, no. I'm an actor. That is to say, I'd like to *be* an actor.

133

On radio. You look like a man on his way up—and I need some advice."

He seemed pleased at my interest in him. "Well, as a matter of fact I've done some voice work on my own. Back where I'm from."

"And where's that, Mr. Corwin?"

"Springfield," he said.

"Ohio?"

"Massachusetts. I was born in Boston, but I started my career in Springfield. I had my own show on WBZA called 'Rhymes and Cadences.' Then, earlier this year, I was an announcer for WLW in Cincinnati. This job here in L.A. is just temporary—until I can put together another show of my own back in Springfield. I'll be producing and directing it."

"Then you think radio has a real future?"

"Absolutely! Radio's been around for a decade now and it's just getting started. There are all kinds of opportunities if a person is willing to pursue them. But it takes dedication."

I nodded. "That's what I am—dedicated." I leaned closer to him on the couch. "You know, I'd really like to talk to a working actor. Somebody who's active in the business. Jeffry Chester, for instance. He's doing a show for you here right now, isn't he?"

"Yes, he is. But I don't know. . . ."

"Could I possibly get in to see him? I'd really appreciate the chance to watch him work. Then, when the show's over, maybe he wouldn't mind if I asked him a question or two. You know, to get his perspective."

Corwin had kind eyes; I knew he was sympathetic and would be willing to help.

"Nobody is supposed to enter the studio when we're broadcasting," he told me. "But perhaps I can make an exception. *If* you'll promise to be very, very quiet."

"Like a mouse," I promised.

"All right, then," Corwin said. "Go through that door where the red light is blinking. But *very* slowly, and *very* quietly."

I shook his hand with a firm, sincere grip, gave him one of my most reassuring smiles, and walked to the door. The blonde was glaring at me, but I ignored her. She started to protest, but Corwin put up a calming hand and I was inside.

Hammett, I told myself, you really *are* an actor.

On the main floor of the studio a trio of performers were gathered in a half-circle around a standing mike, with KFI printed on it in large white letters. Each performer had a script for the show. That's a big plus for radio actors; they don't have to memorize their parts. In the center of the trio was a woman, as large as Kate Smith, with blazing red hair. The actor to her right was a tiny, wizened little gink with a tuft of white beard at his chin. Like a prune with whiskers. To Kate's left was the guy who *had* to be Jeffry Chester. Tall, as skinny as I am, and totally bald. He looked somewhere in his late thirties, wore a baggy gray suit, and his tie was pulled low beneath an open collar.

Off to the far left, a director was giving cues from a glassed booth. A four-man sound effects team worked from their own mikes in a cluttered area directly behind the actors—next to a guy seated at the keys of a big Hammond organ.

Apparently, from what I gathered by their conversation, they'd just finished a timed rehearsal and were about to launch into the actual broadcast. I watched, caught up in the whole thing: I'd never seen live radio.

The director cued the organist and he began working the keys to produce a dolorous theme, suggesting shadows and mystery. Then the wizened little guy took his cue and came in with a rich, highly dramatic baritone voice you'd never figure was inside him: "Welcome . . . to the Castle of Death! . . . where ghosts abound and ancient curses bear dark fruit . . . where prowling demons howl in the night. . . ."

Chester and the redhead howled fiendishly into the mike as the little guy continued: "Come with us down these dank hallways to the Chamber of Horrors . . . where Old Meg slowly stirs her cauldron of blood. . . ." A bubbling effect from the sound men, achieved by hot water boiling in a pan on a portable burner. "Yes! She's waiting for YOU! . . . to tell you the ghastly story of 'The Headless Horseman of Doom!' " A dramatic pause as the organ music peaked. "Welcome to . . . THE WITCH'S CAVERN!"

The red-haired lady let loose with a gust of cackling laughter, ending with a deep: "Hee-hee-hee-hee. . . ." Then, as Old Meg, she began reading from her script in a raspy, cronelike voice: "Greetings, dear hearts! Gather close now . . . closer . . . ah, that's it . . . while I tell ye about my headless friend . . . Hist! I kin hear him now! He's a' comin' he is! Oh, yes! The Horseman of Do-ooo-ooo-mmm!"

A rapping of hollow coconut shells in a box of floor dirt created a fast-galloping horse as the organ added its own pounding beat.

It was Chester's turn. He crouched over the mike and proved that a headless horseman can talk without a head: "All travelers, beware! . . . lest I ride down upon ye from the dark with my sword of death and by one sweep of my blade make ye as *I* am . . . a headless horror!"

It went on in this overcooked vein for the rest of the episode, with each of the three performers playing a variety of roles. Chester was a blind beggar, a terrified innkeeper, a kindly doctor, and a mad dwarf. As different characters, he was killed twice during the broadcast.

And behind it all the hard-working sound effects boys were turning a man inside out (by stripping off a pair of rubber gloves while egg crates were being crushed to simulate snapped bones), making thunder roll (by shaking balloons filled with bird shot), beheading a luckless traveler (a cleaver slicing through a head of lettuce), and creating the sickening sound of a high-falling body smashing to earth (by hurling a soaked rag against a cement slab).

I thought the whole show was ridiculous, but I suppose this sort of lurid melodrama provides certain mush-minded listeners with a half-hour of chills they can't get from the daily newspapers. At least nobody was pretending it was Shakespeare.

With the microphones turned off, I walked in Jeffry Chester's direction. He was talking to the director, who looked weary and beaten; apparently the show hadn't gone to his satisfaction.

"I think you overplayed the mad dwarf," he told Chester.

"I don't agree. He was, after all, *mad*. I'll admit I improvised a bit, but I felt a real emotional rapport with him, so I went with it."

The director looked pained. "All that cackling you added. No good."

"Why no good? I cackle very well."

"Hey, Jeff, I'd never deny you do a terrific cackle. That's not the point."

"Then what *is* the point?"

"It's a matter of balance. Old Meg cackles. She's a witch and that's what she does a lot of. She cackles."

"So?"

"So you can't have a cackling witch and a cackling dwarf on the same show. From now on, let Meg do the cackling."

The director moved away to confer with the sound crew, leaving Chester to me. I introduced myself, giving him my phony name. "Ruth told me to look you up."

He arched an actorish eyebrow. "Ruth?"

"Julio's sister, Ruth Richetti."

He smiled. "Of course. You'll have to forgive me; I know at least three women named Ruth. So—what are you here to see me about?"

"I'm attempting to locate Julio. Ruth said you might know where he is."

"Is he in some kind of trouble? Are you with the law?"

"No to both questions. I'm with Global Studios."

"As what?"

"A film director. We're about to start a new musical. The script's finished and we're into pre-production. Gable's starring for us. It's going to be his first song-and-dance role."

"So what's a musical have to do with Julie?"

"One of our key scenes in the picture is this big dance number. Takes place in the main salon of a gambling ship. Our title, by the way, is *Gamblin' Man*. Like it?"

"I still don't see—"

"We feel it will be to our advantage to shoot the salon number on a real ship. It just wouldn't look authentic on a soundstage. That's where Mr. Richetti comes in."

"Because he now owns the *Lady*?"

"Exactly. Since the craft is not earning Mr. Richetti any money at the moment, being out of commission due to the unfortunate events that resulted in the death of his father, we'd like to take our cameras and crew on board and shoot the dance number there. But, of course, we need Mr. Richetti's permission to do so. We're willing to pay him a handsome sum for the temporary use of his property."

Chester looked dubious. "And Ruthie doesn't know where he is?"

"Not at the moment, no. Seems they've been out of touch. Some kind of family problem."

"Uh-huh." The hook was in the water and he was going for it. "Let's say that I just might know where Julie is. What's in it for me?"

"The studio is prepared to pay what one might term a 'finder's fee' for information that leads us to Mr. Richetti."

"How much?"

"One hundred dollars. Fifty now, and the other fifty when we've found him."

Radio doesn't pay much to character actors and I figured Chester could use the extra money. And while I was plenty tight for cash, I did have the fifty on me. It would be worth it to find Julio.

His Adam's apple was jumping in his skinny neck and I knew I had my fish on the line.

"Did Ruth tell you that we used to hunt together—me and Julie?"

"I think she mentioned it."

"Well, we'd rent this hunting lodge up in the mountains, at Big Bear Lake. Julie liked it so much he bought the place last year. It's in a prime location. Woods all around. Close to the water. Great hunting area."

"And you think he might be there now? At the lodge?"

"It's possible. I mean, he likes to go there to get away from everything. From the hurly-burly, you know."

"Right. I understand."

"And what with all the bad stuff happening on the *Lady*, his old man's getting croaked and the fire and all—my guess is he just decided to cut for the woods."

"Alone?"

"I dunno," said Chester. "Julie usually has a woman with him. Might have one up there."

"Can you tell me how to reach the lodge?"

He smiled, extending a long, skinny hand, palm up. "For fifty down I can."

I smiled back at him and went for my wallet.

FOURTEEN

I'd promised to contact Chandler regarding Julio Richetti. When I phoned him, telling him about the lodge at Big Bear, he was immediately intrigued.

"This fits in exactly with a story I've been planning," Ray declared. "I'm calling it 'The Lady in the Lake.' Most of the plot's worked out, but I need to get up to Big Bear for background research. So there's a double reason for making the trip."

"It's a three-hour drive to the lake," I said. "We can leave tomorrow morning. I'll have Buddy drop me off at your place around seven. How does that sound?"

"Perfect. I'll have the car gassed and ready."

That night, apparently Ray phoned Erle, telling him about our plans, because suddenly we had another passenger. I found Gardner waiting at Ray's house in Santa Monica when I arrived there the next morning.

"I'm going with you," he said. "You *need* me at Big Bear."

"Ray and I can handle this."

"You needed me in Chinatown and you need me now," he argued. "I'm essential."

"He's right," nodded Chandler. "Erle's presence is required."

"Don't tell me *he's* doing a story with a lake setting!"

Erle glared at me. "Will you *listen?*"

"I'm listening."

"I've hunted deer up in those woods," Gardner declared, "with my bow and arrow."

"Like Robin Hood in Sherwood Forest," I said.

"The thing is, I know the terrain. Ray told me where the lodge is, and to reach it we'll need to take a back route around the dam."

"Why a back route?"

"The main road leading into that area is private, with a locked gate. Unless you can prove you live there, the guard won't let you through. But I know another way. The road's a little narrow, but we can make it."

I gave in. "Okay, then, it's the three of us. But we'd better get cracking."

"I don't quite understand what we can expect to accomplish even if Richetti *is* up there," Chandler admitted. "We have no authority to detain him, or even question him. In fact, he could have us arrested for trespassing."

"The deeper I get into this case the more convinced I am that Julio was involved in his father's murder," I told them. "I want to meet Richetti face-to-face and hear his side of it."

"What if he won't talk?" asked Chandler. "What then?"

"If he's innocent, he'll want to refute what Kelly said about him. He'll be anxious to clear himself. If he clams up, then it's a sure sign we're on the right track. And we won't know until we brace him."

Big Bear Lake is in the mountains above San Bernardino and you have to climb a snaking, seven-thousand-foot road to Crestline in order to get there. Ray's big Duesy sailed around the curves with ease: the car was a real class act and Chandler couldn't stop boasting about it. On that steep fifty-mile stretch of twisting road I learned more about the Duesenberg than I cared to know.

"Got this baby in '32," Chandler said. "Eight cylinders. Three hundred twenty horsepower, with a top speed of one thirty. It's the centrifugal supercharger that kicks in the power."

"Impressive," I said, hoping he'd shut up, but he didn't.

"In 1920 a Duesy set the Land Speed Record at Daytona," Ray continued. "One fifty six miles per hour, which was really stepping in those days."

"Uh-huh," I grunted.

"Year later, in '21, Jimmy Murphy won the Grand Prix of France in a Duesenberg," Ray continued. "Only time an American car has ever won a GP race in Europe."

He went on to tell us how the World War I flying ace, Eddie Rickenbacker, drove a Duesy in the Indy 500, winning the race in 1925, along with the AAA Championship, and how the Duesenberg had contributed largely to the general development of the automobile and how these two brothers, Fred and Augie Duesenberg, began working with cars at the turn of the century but that Fred was the true engineering genius. And on and on.

It was a long climb to the top.

We stopped for an early lunch at the Indian Head Hotel, which was part of the village area built for the tourists who flocked here every summer. There was a shooting gallery, dance hall, gas station, post office, some shops designed in imitation Swiss style, a small rustic church and three cafes. But according to Erle, the Indian Head was the only decent place to eat.

The mountain trout were fat and delicious. "Fresh out of Big Bear Lake," the waitress assured us. We topped off the meal with a slab of apple pie that tasted like the kind everybody's mother is supposed to make but usually can't.

Julio's lodge was just three miles from the village if we took the direct route, which we didn't. Erle directed us to a stony dirt road, crowded between high granite boulders and choked with undergrowth, that looped in a large half-circle behind the dam.

"We'll be able to come in just above the lodge," declared Gardner. "We can leave the car there and walk down."

The road was so narrow it looked, for a while, like the big Duesenberg wouldn't be able to squeeze through, but we managed, with Ray cursing every time a tree branch scraped his paint job. The area was totally wild, with spicy-smelling hundred-foot yellow pines shooting up around us. There were thick stands of juniper, plenty of solid black oak trees, and massive bushes of manzanita. We were in the heart of the San Bernardino National Forest. Another world; compared to my usual Hollywood beat, as alien as the far side of the moon.

I could never live up here on any kind of a permanent basis. I need the pulse and roar of a big city around me. All this peace and solitude would eventually drive me loco. A great place to visit, but. . .

Following Erle's instructions, Ray eased the Duesy to a stop in a patch of woods by the side of the road and cut the engine. We were instantly immersed in mountain silence thick enough to swim through. This was the south side of the lake. Big Bear sun-flashed below, with a staggered line of juniper trees marching down to the rock-ribbed shoreline. Above us, white snow drifts frosted the mountaintops, promising a cold winter.

We sat in the car for a long moment, breathing in the deep woods silence. Then Ray asked: "Where's the lodge from here?"

"Directly down this slope about eight hundred yards," Erle replied. Turning to me: "Providing that Jeffry Chester gave you the right location."

"He seemed to know exactly where the place is," I said. "Told me he'd been here half a dozen times with Richetti."

Ray was frowning; he looked agitated.

"What's wrong?" I asked him.

"This Julio character—if he's ducking a possible murder rap he could be very dangerous. We're like a trio of mice stepping into the jaws of a lion."

I shrugged. "If it helps, I'm packing my cannon—and I'm not averse to placing a few round holes in Mr. Richetti should he happen to turn violent on us."

"Shooting a guy in his own home on private property could land you in some very hot water," Erle advised me.

"I promise to keep my trigger finger under control."

"Okay, let's move out," said Erle. "And if you guys get a rip in your pants don't blame me. This is rugged country."

I started down through a heavy tangle of brush, half walking, half sliding. The descent was relatively steep, but I managed to maintain my balance. The .38 snugged under my armpit increased my confidence.

When we reached the bottom of the slope we had a clear view of Big Bear. A scatter of rough-hewn pine cabins dotted the far shore. Several wooden piers fingered out into the water, each with a boat moored to it. The lake itself was a cold ice-blue with nothing to disturb its placid surface. This late in the fall there weren't many active fishermen around and the summer people were long gone. Except for a couple of chittering squirrels, we seemed to have the area pretty much to ourselves.

"There!" exclaimed Erle, pointing to the left. "That's it."

Chester had carefully described Julio's lodge to me and the structure behind a screen of trees to our left fit his description exactly. The place was constructed of milled redwood lined with knotty pine, sunk into a stone foundation, with a steep shingled roof and double garage. A wide porch ran along the lakeside, with a spring-filled reservoir on the hill providing fresh water.

No smoke was visible from the chimney but that figured, even if Richetti was there, since it was still mid-day: the penetrating mountain chill wouldn't set in until sundown.

144

"I don't see any vehicles around," said Ray. To me: "Do you know what Julio drives?"

I shook my head. "Whatever it is, he could have it parked inside the garage."

"Then how can we tell if anybody's home?" Erle asked.

"We'll have to get a lot closer," I said. "If our boy is in there we'll need to surprise him, take him off guard. That way, if he's packing iron, we won't be swallowing bullets for lunch."

"We had *trout* for lunch," Ray corrected me. "But I appreciate the hard lingo. Right out of Sam Spade."

Erle shook his head. "I think we should wait for dark. We'd have a lot better chance of approaching the place without being spotted. And we could be sure he's there if we see lights inside."

"No good," declared Chandler. "I don't want to try navigating that dirt road at night. It's enough of a bitch by daylight. We could end bottom-side up in some canyon."

"Ray's right," I said. "Besides, I want to get this show on the road. We're here now—so we go now."

Erle nodded. "Okay, I'm outvoted."

Now Ray was hesitating. Neither one of them liked the idea of bracing Richetti head-to-head, and I didn't like it much myself, but I couldn't see anything else to do.

"Let's say we spot him inside the house," said Chandler. "Maybe through a window. Wouldn't it make sense to call in the authorities at that point?"

"Authorities?" I looked sour. "If you mean the cops, they're not going to do a damn thing. There's no warrant out for Richetti. Apparently, we're the only ones who have him pegged for his papa's wipeout, and we're still investigating that aspect. He could be totally in the clear. So—to answer your question, Ray, *no*, it wouldn't make sense to call in anybody. This is our little show till the curtain goes down."

"Hopefully not on us," muttered Gardner.

Keeping low and moving cautiously, we started for the lodge.

145

There was something a bit absurd about three grown men creeping through the brush toward the house of a stranger who might or might not be a cold-blooded killer. But creep we did, circling the lodge and coming in at an angle which brought us to the rear of the structure. When we reached one of the back windows and peered inside, no alarms went off, no savage dogs were unleashed, and no shouts or shots came from the house. In fact, everything was mountain-quiet.

A rear window gave us our view of the kitchen and pantry area. Deserted. Separating, we each moved to a side window, through which we could see the main rooms in the front section of the one-story building. No sound. No movement. Nothing. Unless he was hiding under the bed, Julio Richetti did not appear to be in residence.

"Well," said Chandler. "It looks as if we came all this way for—"

I cut him off with a raised hand. "Wait," I said. "I hear something."

We all held our breath, listening intently to a faint humming sound.

"It's coming from the garage," Erle said.

I slipped out my .38, on a just-in-case basis, and we eased up to a service door. I tried the knob. Unlocked. Opening it, we ducked quickly inside. The door to the attached garage was also unlocked. Taking the lead, I jerked it wide, gun up and ready.

A stinging surge of blue-gray smoke drove us back. The place reeked of poisonous fumes. A new canary-yellow Chrysler Custom Imperial was inside the garage, its engine running. A hose extended from the car's exhaust pipe through the passenger window, into the front seat. Someone was inside, head down, eyes closed. A female someone. Young, blonde, and unconscious.

As Chandler got the garage door open, choking back the

noxious fumes, I cut the ignition and scooped up the girl. Her head flopped to one side and I wasn't sure she was still alive. She was in a wrinkled cornflower-blue dress and one of her beige high-heeled shoes fell off as I carried her outside. Finally, I could see that she was breathing. Good thing we hadn't waited until dark. Otherwise, I'd have been hauling out a corpse.

I let her slip from my arms to the grass near the porch steps. She was quite attractive, her beauty unflawed except for a small mole on her left cheek. The three of us crowded around her as she sat up, coughing violently. "What—what happened? Who are you?"

"Don't try to talk," I told her. "Give your lungs a chance to take in some clean air." To Gardner: "Go to the kitchen and bring her water."

After drinking from the glass she was able to talk.

"I'm Jean Adams. Who are you? What's going on?"

"We found you in the car," I told her. "With the engine running and an exhaust hose in the window. Why did you try to kill yourself?"

"But I *didn't*! He must have done it, and tried to make it look like suicide. That filthy—"

"You're talking about Julio Richetti?" I asked.

"Yes!" She scrubbed at the tears in her eyes with Erle's white handkerchief. "He wanted me dead."

"Why?" Erle wanted to know. "Why would Richetti try to kill you?"

Her nostrils flared. "Because I know he did it, and I told him so."

"Did what?"

"Killed his father and that other woman. With a machine gun." She shuddered. "But I didn't tell anybody. I thought Julio loved me. He kept swearing it. He said he was going to take me to Europe as soon as he got some really big money."

147

"From the Cat's Eye," I said. "Did you know about the jeweled skull?"

"Yes. Julio's father had it in the stateroom that night. That's the reason Julio killed him—to get the skull. But that's the last time I saw it. Julio took it to someone to sell, but I don't know who."

"Did he force you to come up here to Big Bear with him?" Erle asked.

"No, no. . . ." Her face was strained and her eyes were red-veined and desperate. "I *wanted* to be with him. He kept telling me how much I meant to him, that he couldn't live without me, and I believed him. I really thought he loved me." She looked down at her trembling hands. "But he was just playing me for a fool."

I needed to know a lot more. "What happened after you got up here to the lodge?"

"It was fine for a while. It was like . . . like kind of a honeymoon, I guess you could say. Julio was very sweet and gentle with me. Then, this morning, we had this terrible argument."

I kept pressing. "What about?"

"About getting married. I was ashamed of the way we'd been living. Even though I loved him, I said we couldn't go on this way, that it made me feel dirty. I said I'd leave him if he didn't marry me—and he got furious. No woman was ever going to chain him down, he said. I told him I'd go to the police and tell them everything unless he promised to marry me. He asked if I'd really do that, and I said I would, that I still loved him but I wouldn't be just another one of his women."

"What happened then?" I asked.

"He seemed to get a lot calmer. He said that I was right, that it was time for him to settle down, and that yes, we'd get married just as soon as we got back to L.A. He said he was sorry he'd lost his temper and asked me to forgive him. He hugged me and everything—and I believed him all over again. I guess because I

148

wanted to so much. Then he said, 'Let's have a toast to our future wedding.' And that's when he must have put something in my drink, maybe some sleeping powder. Anyway, the next thing I remember is waking up out here on the grass." She looked at all of us. "You saved my life. I'd be dead if you hadn't come along when you did."

Erle touched her shoulder. "Where's Julio now?"

"I don't know. He was driving his Packard; a maroon Packard. That's what we came here in. The Chrysler was already in the garage. He kept it here at the lodge so we'd each have a car."

I wrote down a description of the Packard, but she couldn't recall the license number.

Big Bill Kelly had told the truth; Richetti *was* the killer.

"I'm parked up on the hill," Chandler told her. "We'll drive you back to L.A. with us."

She shook her head. "No, I want to take the Chrysler. I can get some gas in the village. The thing is, I just need to be alone. To kind of pull myself together. I'll meet you wherever you say tomorrow, but I need some time to myself tonight. Can you understand that?"

I told her okay, we understood, but to be careful. She was now a key witness. "You'll be asked to testify against Richetti once he's found."

"I know. And I want to. I want to tell the truth," she said, nodding firmly. "I want Julio to pay for those killings and for what he tried to do to me."

What I didn't tell her was that she was also an accessory to murder, but the DA would, no doubt, make a deal with her in exchange for her testimony. The important thing was to get her on the stand.

I gave her my Pacific Palisades address, and told her to be there at noon tomorrow.

"All right," she agreed. "At noon."

* * *

Jean Adams didn't show up the next day. She *had* been there during the night, long enough to leave a pink envelope, smelling faintly of lilac perfume, tacked to my door. There was a hand-written letter inside, on pink stationery:

Dear Mr. Hammett,

I'm so very sorry that I couldn't meet you as I promised. But after thinking things over I have come to a big decision. I've made up my mind that I have to go back to where I came from—to Minnesota—and try and forget all the horrible things that have happened to me here in California. As much as I want to see Julio sent to prison, I just can't face going to the police and testifying in a murder trial and all the rest of it. I'm just not strong enough to bear this kind of pressure and strain right now. I'm certain that I'd have a nervous breakdown. I hope you'll forgive me and not think badly of me. I owe you and your friends my life and I shall never forget what the three of you did for me. But I *can't* stay in Los Angeles. Not now. I'm going home.

Sincerely,
and with my deepest
gratitude,
Jean Adams

P.S. Please don't try to find me. Minnesota is a big state and you would just be wasting your time.
J.A.

FIFTEEN

I phoned Erle and Ray when I read Jean's note and we agreed to meet at Musso's. Over coffee and lemon cream pie, we all came to the same frustrating conclusion: we'd reached another dead end in the case. Julio had vanished; the Cat's Eye had vanished; and our star witness had vanished. Three for three.

Unofficially, Jean Adams was a fugitive from justice, but there was no way to bring her back to Los Angeles even if she *could* be found in the vastness of Minnesota. As far as the ship killings were concerned, we now knew who pulled the trigger, but nobody in law enforcement would believe us, or act on what we said, so what good did our knowledge do? When Jean Adams left town, our proof left with her.

"Are we just going to let Julio get away with pulling off a double murder and the theft of the Cat's Eye?" Chandler asked me.

My answer was flat and final: "You bet we are. We can't do a damn thing at this point and you know it."

Erle agreed with me. We were at a complete standstill.

And I had a living to make and bills to pay, including Buddy's overdue salary, so I knew I had to find some screen work fast.

The answer to my dilemma came from a completely unexpected source: Ernest Hemingway.

Hem wanted to see me. He was in town because a producer named Gunther Flood had paid his way out here from Key West. Hem claimed that he was offered a big chunk of money for the screen rights to his boxing story "Fifty Grand," and did *I* want a shot at writing the script?

"You know what I think of this screen stuff," he told me over the phone. "Hollywood's as phony as a wooden doughnut. Movies are horseshit. When it comes to writing for the studios, I'm not their boy, but I sure don't mind collecting some of their loose dough while I'm in town, providing I don't have to do anything but stick out my mitt to collect it."

"We have to talk about this," I said. "Where are you staying?"

"In one of these frigging chicken coops at the Garden," he growled. I knew he meant the Garden of Allah Hotel on Sunset, at the foot of the Hollywood hills. Twenty-five tile-roofed bungalows sunk in tropical shrubbery, circling a huge, lotus-shaped swimming pool. A lot of writers, actors, and producers rented the shabbily maintained bungalows (the hotel called them "villas"), and naked starlets were regularly tossed into the pool. A place of passion and high drama, the Garden's history included rapes, robberies, drunken brawls, wild parties, attempted suicides, and at least one kidnapping.

Hemingway was staying in Bungalow 10, on the far side of the parking lot, and as I moved over the narrow stone pathway between dust-layered bamboo and banana trees I wondered why he'd chosen to stay at the Garden; it didn't seem to suit his personality.

That was the first question I asked him when I shook his hairy paw in the doorway of Bungalow 10.

"Hell, I didn't pick out this joint," he growled. "Flood reserved it for me. Errol Flynn's got the bungalow next door and he spent most of last night banging some broad, with the two of 'em rutting away like a couple of hyenas. Damn walls are so thin you can hear a flea fart. Naturally, I didn't get much shut-eye."

He was stubble-bearded, in khaki, with a safari jacket over the bulge of his stomach. A long-billed fishing cap shaded his eyes.

We went inside and Hemingway shut the door, walked over to a glass coffee table in the corner of the room, and made himself a tall drink from an array of gin, bourbon, and Scotch bottles. I told him I'd settle for ice water.

"Jesus, Hammett, if you don't *drink* out here, what the crap *do* you do?"

I shrugged the question aside and settled into one of the heavy Spanish chairs. It looked old enough to have served during the Inquisition.

The room was less than charming. The rose carpet had faded to vomit gray and the cracked walls had been painted a pale apple green a long, long time ago. A dim, crudely executed painting of an early California mission hung over the couch; the oak frame was chipped and peeling.

Drink in hand, Hemingway paced the room like an angry bear. In the years I'd known him—and we'd seen each other socially maybe half a dozen times—he was always sore about something. He had a particular bias against literary critics; even when they *liked* his stuff he found cause to grouse about their reviews.

"This Flood guy practically wept crocodile tears when I told him I didn't write movies. I guess he expected me to sit down in front of him and whomp out a script. Producers give me a pain in the gut. They don't understand writers."

"That's for sure," I agreed.

"I told Flood I'd sell him the screen rights to my story so long as I didn't have to adapt it. Told him he should hire you for the job. In fact, I told him that if he *didn't* hire you, I wouldn't sell him the goddam rights!"

"That was loyal of you, Hem."

"Loyal, my ass! I'm just trying to protect the material. I don't want my name connected with another fucking abomination. Did you see the way they crapped up *Arms?*"

He meant the 1932 production of *A Farewell to Arms*, based on his novel, and starring Gary Cooper. Frank Borzage had directed it for Paramount. Hemingway's face reddened as he recalled the film.

"Coop was okay, but the script was all screwed up. They even had Catherine *survive* the hospital!"

Hemingway's tragic heroine, Catherine Barkley, pregnant with the hero's child, dies in the hospital at the end of the book, but this was too downbeat for Paramount. They had indeed "crapped it up."

I asked him about Flood's reaction to his demand that I be hired for the new film. Hem snorted, smiling crookedly. "This fathead loves boxing and he tells me that my 'Fifty Grand' is the best prizefight story ever written, which is okay because he happens to be right. Anyhow, he wants the story real bad, so he said fine, he'd hire you if you were available."

"I'm available. I'm *very* available."

"Then you'll do it?"

"Gladly," I said.

"Do you remember the story?"

"Been a while since I read it, but I seem to recall you based it on a real fight."

"Right," he said, draining his glass. He fixed another drink as he talked. "On the welterweight championship bout in New York back in twenty-two between Leonard and Britton. Benny Leonard was hot after the title and in the thirteenth round he fouled Jack Britton, who was then the welterweight king. So Jack won on the foul. When I wrote my story I switched things around some and worked in a double cross."

"I remember now," I said. "Story's a peach. Should make a dandy movie."

"Yeah, well, that's your department," he said, knocking off the second glass. He lumbered over to the corner table to fix himself another. I never did get my ice water.

I knew that Hemingway fancied himself as a potent amateur boxer, though he'd never had any pro fights. He was something of a character back in Key West where he'd pledged to pay two hundred and fifty dollars to any local who could last three rounds with him. So far, he hadn't paid out a dime. His chest and arm muscles were powerfully developed from the constant strain of hauling in the giant marlin he regularly hooked in the Gulf Stream and he wasn't an easy man to knock down.

We got to talking fights and fighters as Hem lounged back on the couch and worked on another drink. He bragged that he'd "done plenty okay" during four exhibition rounds in the ring with Tom Heeney. "I even hurt him a little."

I said that I didn't recognize the name.

"Jeez, he fought Gene Tunney once! The guy's from New Zealand. A mean heavyweight and a real tough professional. Not like that cowardly son of a bitch Max Baer."

Why did he have such contempt for Baer?

"Last September I was in New York to cover the heavyweight championship for *Esquire*," he told me in a sullen, booze-fogged voice. "Baer against Louis."

"Sure, I know all about that one," I said. "Ended in the fourth round when Baer was counted out."

"Joe Louis is one damn beautiful fighting machine," Hem declared, finishing his drink. "Baer was scared shitless in there with Louis. I could smell the fear on him at ringside, like the stink that comes off a dying animal."

Before I could comment on this, Hemingway lurched to his feet, hamlike fists clenched, crouching and feinting at me. "Get up, Hammett, and let's see what you're made of."

I stood up from the chair, grinning uncomfortably. "I don't

box," I said, aware that Hemingway was suddenly drunk and dangerous.

"You chicken?" he demanded.

"No, but I'm not a boxer," I said, keeping my voice calm and level. "I've had a few roughups in my time, but I could never match you, Ernest."

"I say you're chicken!" he growled, coming at me with fire in his eyes. His face was flushed and sweat-beaded.

I backed away from him, easing toward the door.

"Stand still and fight, you yellow-livered pansy!" shouted Hemingway, putting his full weight into a roundhouse right that, had it landed, would likely have put me in the hospital.

I was able to duck under it, with the blow whistling past my jaw. Totally unbalanced, carried forward by his own momentum, Hemingway smashed his fist through the wall, gouging a sizable dent in the plaster.

The drunken boxer fell to his knees on the carpet, sucking at his bleeding right hand.

"Talk to you later, Hem," I said, walking quickly out the door. Behind me, inside the bungalow, I heard the big man groaning and cursing.

I figured I could kiss my latest screen job good-bye.

Two days later I got a handwritten note from Hemingway. It surprised me. Not only did he apologize for what he termed his "really blackass behavior," but he also gave me Flood's personal phone number and told me to call him. "He's a hundred percent sold on you," Hemingway wrote, "and the assignment is yours if you still want it."

Naturally, I did—and made an appointment that same morning to see Flood at Fox, where he was shooting his latest film.

Buddy drove me over.

Knives upset me. Always have. I can handle guns, emotionally speaking. They're an acceptable risk. I've used guns on people

156

and people have used guns on me. I've got the scars to prove it. But I have never carried a knife; the thought of being stabbed, of having a sharp blade slice into my flesh, severing arteries, cutting through nerves and muscles and tissue, engenders a kind of whirling sickness in the pit of my stomach.

That's why I was nervous about the two knife-wielding characters, one tall and one squat, who were squaring off in front of me. Not that I was personally threatened. So far as I could tell, they didn't even know I was there. It was just the idea of these two hard-faced mugs cutting each other up with abandon that put me off.

And this was no dream, like Kelly and the elephant. This was real. The tall guy was dressed in a neat pin-striped suit and the squat one wore dark pants, a scuffed leather jacket, and work boots.

"You been askin' for this," said the tall one, acid in his tone. "Now you're gonna get what you been askin' for." He was gripping a wide-bladed woodsman's hunting knife, the kind you skin animals with, and he moved toward his shorter opponent with head lowered, like a bull.

"I ain't scared a' you," said the squat man. "And we'll see who gets what before this is over." His knife had a thinner, longer blade—a wicked-looking job he'd pulled from his right boot.

From the easy way they handled their blades, I could see they were veterans at this sort of business.

They circled each other like wary jungle cats. Then the tall man said: "Get ready to die, Bennie. I'm gonna open you up from your liver to your lights."

Bennie didn't back off at this. In fact, he took the offensive, darting in on the tall man and slashing at his body.

A welter of crimson darkened the tall man's chest, staining his pin-striped suit as Bennie's blade struck home. The tall man grunted, dropped the hunting knife, and staggered back, his eyes shocked and wide.

157

"You stinkin' little runt!" he gasped through a sudden bubble of red at his lips. "You've gone and—done me in!"

Then he collapsed forward like a wet sack, sprawling to the concrete walk.

"Cut!" yelled Gunther Flood, walking over to the fallen actor. "You bit down too soon on the capsule, Fred," he told the tall man. "We're not supposed to see any blood on your lips till the camera dollies in for your close-up. *Then* you bite down and we get our blood. What the hell were you thinking about?"

"I'm really sorry, Gunther," the tall man said, looking sheepish as he stood up. "I just got lost in the scene and forgot what you'd told me about when to bite down. I mean, I must have done it kind of *instinctive*-like."

"All right, we'll get you a change of wardrobe and pick this up again after lunch," said Flood.

"What about me?" asked the squat man. "Did I do okay? Was it what you wanted?"

Actors are like scared kids, they always need a reassuring word from their director. They need to be coddled, and these two were no different. A couple of tough-looking mugs begging to be told they did okay.

"You were swell," said Flood. "You were both swell. The whole scene was swell. One more take after lunch and we'll have it wrapped."

The two actors left the set, arm in arm, as the assistant director called "Lunch!" to the rest of the crew.

Flood walked over to me through a licorice-tangle of fat black electrical power cables. "Well, what did you think? You've seen plenty of knife fights. Was this one real?"

"Real enough to make me queasy," I told him. "I've never liked knives."

"The little guy is a dock worker who refuses to kick in to the union bosses, so they send the tall guy to cut him up, only the

158

little guy comes out on top and it's the tall guy who buys it. Neat switch, eh?"

"What's your title?"

"*Blood on the Waterfront.* You think it's too lurid?"

"Nope." I shook my head. "Sounds like solid box office."

Flood was compact and bearded. He had a round face and his heavily pouched eyes testified to the lack of sleep he kept complaining about. Directors work hard; he was probably lining up the next day's action each night when he should have been in the sack.

Now he took my elbow and steered me toward an exit door. "We'll eat in my trailer," he said. "That okay with you?"

"Fine."

Parked just outside the sound stage, Flood's trailer was as long as a dirigible and furnished like a bordello. Gold chairs. Gold tables. Mirrors with gold frames. Walls flocked in red velvet.

"Got all this stuff from the prop department," he said proudly. "Really dresses up the place. Makes it look kinda *regal*, doncha know."

"Yeah," I nodded. "Like your own little palace on wheels."

Flood smiled, pressed a button near the door, and—a few moments later—a studio slave entered with our lunch: tomato soup, an impressive salad of mixed vegetables and sesame seeds, grilled vegetables over rice, and fruit salad for dessert. There were also some tasty hot sourdough rolls that reminded me nostalgically of long-ago meals in San Francisco.

"I'm not a meat eater," Flood told me around a mouthful of asparagus. "Don't like the idea of devouring a dead animal. Meat is decomposing flesh, you know."

"To each his own," I said.

"Take bacon and eggs," he went on. "Bacon is just a cover word for dead pig flesh. If people had to order it that way, if they had to ask for 'dead pig,' you'd see a big change in breakfast

159

habits. Then all these innocent pigs wouldn't be getting their throats cut. Pigs are gentle, loving creatures. They don't belong on your breakfast plate."

"You've got a point there," I said, finishing my salad. I had to hand it to him, he ordered great salads.

"I guess you want to talk about the Hemingway project," he said.

"That's what I'm here for."

"The trouble with Ernest is his dialogue," declared Flood. "Reads okay on a printed page, but it doesn't translate worth a damn to the screen. It's crappy and artificial."

"I thought you wanted Hemingway to do the script," I said. "Isn't that why you brought him out here from Florida?"

"So I made a mistake." Flood was vigorously chewing his broccoli. "More I think about it, the happier I am to have you on this picture. You write good snappy dialogue. That *Thin Man* stuff between Nick and Nora, that's balls out!"

"Like it, huh?" I was deep into the green beans.

"Absolutely perfecto for the silver screen," he said, wiping his mouth with a large red napkin lined in gold. "Now, with this Hemingway thing, I want to expand the original, open it up, get it out of a sweaty gym and into the heart and pulsebeat of a big city."

I nodded. "Like making a mountain out of a molehill."

"Exactly!"

"But it *is* going to be about boxing?" I asked, uncertain of just how far he wanted to go with his changes.

"Sure, sure, you bet," Flood declared. "Big Bill envisions this one as an *epic* of the prize ring!"

"Big Bill?"

"Our executive producer," said Flood. "The guy who's putting up a fat chunk of the money for this picture—Big Bill Kelly."

At that particular moment I was swallowing a carrot.

I almost choked on it.

SIXTEEN

Life is often ironic. I decided to stay with the Flood script assignment, even though it was being bankrolled by Kelly, because I desperately needed the money. In expanding his business interests to include moviemaking, Big Bill apparently didn't mind me being his script writer. At least he never talked about me to Flood, and I didn't talk to Flood about him.

I gave "Fifty Grand" my best shot. But, according to Flood, I missed the target.

"I see this in a different light," he told me after I'd turned in my final draft of the script. "You just don't seem to have the *feel* for Hemingway."

"I've read everything he's written," I said. "You'll never find anybody else who—"

"I'm not looking for anybody else," Flood cut in. "This needs my personal touch—to give it intense depth of emotion. I'll do the script myself."

"Have you ever written a screenplay?"

"What difference does *that* make?" He looked flushed and angry.

And that's exactly what he did. He scripted it himself.

As an example of why directors who have never written screenplays should, lacking the requisite talent, never write screenplays, I herewith reproduce the final scene from Gunther Flood's version of "Fifty Grand."

INTERIOR LOCKER ROOM—NIGHT

They carry Jack into the room and drop him on the rubbing table. He looks awful.

> JACK
> I lost the fight and I look awful.

Jack's handler, Soapy, looks down at him.

> SOAPY
> You look awful, Jack.

Janey, her two eyes popping, runs in. She throws her two arms around Jack.

> JANEY
> You lost the fight but you won my heart, you big lug, you!

> JACK
> You're like a glorious ray of buttery yellow sunshine in a dark room! . . . You're like a fall of gentle rain on a parched desert!

> JANEY
> Kiss me, Jack. Oh, kiss me till my lips fall off!

They kiss like two crazed animals, thrashing about on the rubbing table.

> JACK
> I'm giving up the fight game for you, Janey.

We'll get married and have six kids and a
white picket fence.

JANEY

Hold me, Jack! Crush me!

JACK

Oh, Janey!

JANEY

Oh, Jack!

*And, as they crush one another in unbridled passion, we
CLOSE on a bluebird singing for joy outside the window.*

END

At least Flood took my name off the thing when it went to the
studio, who sent it along to Hemingway in Key West for his
reaction.

And he *did* react.

Hem sent back a letter threatening to tear down the studio
with his two bare hands and also to yank out Flood's genitals if
they went ahead and produced the film.

I had a final meeting with Flood in his trailer. He looked awful.

"It would seem that Ernest failed to appreciate the intense
depth of emotion you achieved with your script," I said.

"It would seem so," he agreed.

And that ended it.

I had no regrets. Hem was sore at Flood, not me, and I'd made
enough green out of the job to pay off my bills and supply Buddy
with all of his back salary. The fact that Big Bill Kelly was
involved in the financial end of this aborted project merely
proved once again that life is often ironic.

That same weekend I got a call from Erle which put me back
on the trail of the Cat's Eye.

"I think I know where the skull is," he said.

"Somewhere in Europe?"

"Nope," Erle told me with triumph in his voice. "It's smack under our noses."

"Where?"

"Right here in Los Angeles. In a shop on Alvarado, near downtown."

"How do you know?"

"Contact of mine, a smalltimer named Erb Yellin, put me onto it. He tells me about this Greek curio shop owner, name of Papadopoulos, who buys on a regular basis from him."

"Drugs?" I asked.

"Yeah, Erb's a supplier."

"Go on."

"Anyhow, this Papadopoulos tells my man that he expects to make a big killing real soon. Says he's handling the sale of this jeweled skull for a special client."

"Said client being our pal Julio Richetti."

"Has to be. Only, natch, the Greek guy keeps mum on who his client is, and ole Erb, he doesn't know anything about the skull's history, or even what it's called."

"Gotcha," I said.

"So the Greek brags to Erb that when he wraps up the sale he'll be getting a big cut of the money. Not too smart, if you ask me, shooting off his mouth to a lowlife like Yellin."

"But it's a break for us."

"Oh, definitely."

"Does Yellin know for certain if the Greek still has the skull?"

"He still has it. Told Erb that the sale is due to happen sometime next week."

"What about the Greek's address?"

"I looked it up. The place is on Alvarado, just short of Wilshire."

"I'll have Buddy take us there. Pick you up in half an hour."

"What do you plan to do?" Erle asked me. "We can't just bust in and grab the Eye."

"It's stolen property. The Greek has no legal right to sell it."

"Fine. You know it and I know it, but how do we convince *him*?"

"I'll describe it, sight unseen. Then, to verify, he can phone Shaw in New York."

"That won't be enough," said Erle. "He'll never turn a valuable thing like that over to us based on a description and a phone call."

"Maybe not, but at least he can lead us to Julio and that's our start."

The Greek's shop was exactly where Erle said it would be—on Alvarado just a few doors north of Wilshire, sandwiched between Fred's Econo-Cleaners and a place called The Lazy Bookworm that sold back-issue pulp magazines six for a quarter and used books for a half-buck each. I know that because the prices were marked on window cards.

Buddy parked in an alley off the street, staying with the limo while Erle and I approached the curio shop. It was late afternoon and our long shadows stepped out with us as we moved over the sidewalk. The two big display windows facing Alvarado were filled with the usual array of clocks, antique chairs, old rugs, ugly tassled lamps, and a number of dusty vases arranged on a long table that looked as if it might have come from a Benedictine monastary.

A printed sign told us that the shop was open till 6 P.M. so I assumed that Papadopoulos himself would come out to greet his newest customers. I even had an opening line prepared for him: "We're interested in looking at jeweled skulls." Just to see his jaw drop.

A little bronze bell above the door jangled as we entered. The place was semi-dark inside; the waning afternoon sun wasn't fully penetrating its interior and I had to adjust my eyes to the dimness.

We waited—but nobody emerged from the shadowy rear of the shop. There was only a heavy silence, thick as an antique Greek rug.

I broke it by walking to the counter and palming the hand bell: bing-bing-bing-bing.

Nothing. Just more rug-thick silence.

Erle looked nervous. "I don't get this. Yellin said that Papadopoulos is always here during working hours. Runs the shop alone because he doesn't trust anybody else."

"Then where is he?"

"Beats me."

"Well, *some*body's got to be here." And I gave a yell.

Nothing.

"C'mon," I said. "Let's have a look in back."

We walked behind the counter, ducking through a rustling curtain of Greek beads, to the rear of the shop.

Papadopoulos was waiting for us there. Dressed in a pressed gray herringbone suit and buttoned vest. A silver stickpin held his striped tie neatly in place. His blackened eyes were staring at us. A shiny fat bluebottle fly was crawling slowly over the bridge of his nose. He didn't brush it away, just kept staring at us. Which figured. When you're dead, flies don't bother you.

"Looks like somebody got here before we did," I said.

"Jesus!" said Gardner.

Papadopoulos was sitting in a high-backed antique chair. He had a small round hole in the center of his forehead.

"Go up front and phone the cops," I said. "Give 'em the address, but don't identify yourself. By the time they get here, we'll be gone."

Erle blinked at me.

"Go ahead, I want to look around a little."

"Do you think whoever killed him got the Cat's Eye?"

I grinned. "Does a bear shit in the woods?"

Gardner nodded and left to call in some law.

What I was looking for in Papa's shop was an address for Julio Richetti. But I had no luck in finding it and we had to leave the place empty-handed.

The cops turned up more than we did. In a trash barrel behind the shop they found a gun which tied directly to the killing. One round had been fired and it matched the hole in Papa's head.

This latest wipe-out was headlined the next day, along with a photo of the murder weapon: a pearl-handled collector's .45 Colt with the initials JR stamped into the barrel. It was known that Julio Richetti was a gun collector and the police had received word from an anonymous source that he'd been doing some drug business with the Greek. That same afternoon a warrant was issued for Julio's arrest.

The whole thing was an obvious frame. Julio himself would never have left the gun there. With a big sale for the Cat's Eye just over the horizon, Richetti would have no reason to murder the man who was setting up the deal. Somebody else found out about the skull and used Julio's gun to kill the Greek, heist the Eye, and alert the cops, conveniently dumping the Colt to provide evidence that Julio was the killer.

My money was on Big Bill Kelly. The Greek's bragging to Yellin had cost him his life. When word got back to Kelly that Papadopoulos had the Eye, he set up the frame. More irony here, since Julio had tried to frame Kelly for the ship murders. Tit for tat. At least this was the way I doped it out and Ray and Erle agreed. Now the question was: would the cops be able to find Julio?

It didn't take long to get the answer to that one.

The same somebody (read Kelly) who killed Papadopoulos

made an anonymous phone call to police headquarters, supplying an address, and a hatful of gun-happy cops swarmed all over a downtown apartment house on Flower. Julio was inside, in a top-floor apartment, but he wasn't in any shape to be arrested; they found him hanging from an overhead pipe in the bathroom. Naturally, the coroner pronounced it suicide—which verified that Julio had done the killing on Alvarado. Guilt over his action had prompted the hanging.

Which was bull. It was Kelly's doing; I was dead certain he was the one and that he now had the Cat's Eye. But, again, there was no way to prove anything against him. Back to square one.

A maddening game.

I felt that it was time for me to act on my own. There was no use involving Gardner or Chandler in what I was about to attempt.

Kelly was having a private lawn party at his Beverly Hills mansion the following Friday night to celebrate his daughter's engagement to some real estate hotshot from Philadelphia. I decided to attend. The shindig was by printed invitation only, but that didn't present a problem. Among my contacts was an ex-counterfeiter-turned-printer named Jack Maclay who could whip up a fake invitation quicker than a cat can shake its whiskers.

But first I had to get a look at one of the invitations. I figured Kelly would be inviting his producer, Gunther Flood, and I was right. We arranged to meet in his trailer on the pretext of my coming in to pitch a film idea. During the course of our meeting I got around to the subject of Big Bill, and Flood proudly showed me his invitation to the party. After that it was easy. I was able to describe it exactly for Maclay, right down to the typeface and paper thickness. I retain stuff like this—another by-product of my years with Pinkerton. As a detective, you've got to remember a lot of odd things, details that can end up saving your life.

"I'll have it ready by Friday morning," Jack promised.

My next stop was the makeup department at Global. I knew a gal who worked there and, under the pretense of taking her to lunch, I was able to swipe a false beard and a pair of thick-lensed glasses. Just to be sure Kelly didn't spot me in the crowd. And naturally I had the invitation made out to Peter Collinson.

Pete was back in business again.

Kelly's place was on Sunset, just before the boulevard starts winding toward Brentwood, and Buddy drove me over. We rolled up to a tall black iron gate edged in gold. The uniformed guard, all smiles, walked over to us.

"Invitation, please."

I handed him the card. Glancing briefly at it, he nodded: "Ah, yes, Mr. Collinson." His smile was dazzling. "It's straight up. You make a left turn at the crest."

He waved us through and we drove up the long curve of the hill, taking a left at the top. I got out of the car as Buddy prepared to drive into the assigned parking area reserved for chauffeured limos.

He leaned from the driver's window: "Chief, I don't know what you're up to, but it's probably something dangerous, so try not to get yourself killed. It's like you said—the Depression's on and I need the work."

"I'll keep that in mind."

Most of the guests had arrived and the lawn was packed with women in designer gowns and men in full-dress tuxedos. I wore the tux I'd long ago borrowed from Global's wardrobe department. It made me look dignified and dapper; the beard and glasses helped.

A waiter in white drifted by and I accepted a glass of wine from his tray. Then I mingled with the other guests, keeping a sharp eye peeled for Big Bill. My disguise was good, but I didn't want to risk a direct, face-to-face confrontation with Kelly.

169

I had a wild plan—to enter the main house through the kitchen, locate Kelly's office, and open his wall safe in hopes of finding the Cat's Eye inside. I knew my chances were slim to none, that he might be keeping the skull on board the *Horseshoe*, or that it might already be sold, but I had to try. Nothing ventured, nothing gained.

I'd opened quite a few safes with Pinkerton and possessed what my colleagues had called a "magic ear." Meaning I could mark the fall of a tumbler with uncanny accuracy. A handy talent. If things ever got really tough in Hollywood I could always make my living as a professional safecracker.

Of course, there was no way to know if I'd be able to crack Kelly's safe until I got to it. One thing at a time. Right now, I needed to find the kitchen. I was moving toward the rear of the mansion when a woman's querulous voice stopped me.

"Don't I know you?"

I turned to smile blankly into the seamed face of Bill Kelly's mother. I'd seen her photo on Kelly's desk on board the *Horseshoe*, so right away I knew who she was. She had to be in her seventies. Tall, like her son, with sharply inquisitive eyes. The gown she wore must have cost a small fortune.

She might have seen my picture in the papers, but surely she couldn't recognize me behind the beard and glasses.

"I'm Peter Collinson," I told her. "Professor Collinson, actually. From the University of California at Berkeley. I teach there."

She shook her head, frowning. "Somehow, you look familiar, but perhaps I'm mistaken. What is it that you teach?"

"Ah . . . classical verse." It was the first thing that popped into my head and I hoped it didn't sound too phony. "From Sappho . . . to Shakespeare . . . to, ah, *other* classics."

"My, my," she clucked. "I'm a poet myself. Amateur, of course."

"Of course," I said. "I mean, I understand."

I was floundering, desperate to break off the conversation. She could call her son over any second for introductions and the jig would be up.

I checked my wristwatch. "Really, I must be—"

Too late. She launched directly into a highly dramatic recital of one of her poems: "Oh, fresh spring clouds in heavens bright, I glory in thy awesome flight. Let thy beauty bind me, mind and heart, and never from thee shall I depart."

She studied me with narrowed eyes. "Tell me truthfully, Professor, have I the precious gift of verse?"

"I would certainly say so," I told her. "It's just a matter of work and refinement. That's what I tell my students—work and refinement."

"I'm touched," she declared. "That a man of your stature would approve one of my humble efforts—I'm truly touched."

"Well, I—"

"Would you care to hear another of my poems?"

"I'd love to," I said, consulting my watch again, "but unhappily I have an urgent appointment and I'm already late. Would you be kind enough to excuse me?"

"By all means, Professor Collinson. I *so* enjoyed our little chat. Perhaps you could visit us in the future."

"What a lovely idea," I said, giving her a warm smile and a quick nod before I hurriedly stepped away.

I'd reached the back patio and was moving toward an open kitchen door when I felt a hand on my shoulder. Surely not Mrs. Kelly again?

"Hey, pal, your beard's falling off."

I was facing one of Big Bill's security guards and he looked meaner than a hungry bulldog. I groped at my sagging beard. Damn that studio spirit gum! I should have used glue.

He kept his hand firmly planted on my shoulder. "Let's see some ID pronto."

"Leave that man alone!" Mrs. Kelly rushed up to us, enraged

171

that I was being detained. "He is Professor Peter Collinson of the University of California at Berkeley and he has an urgent appointment!"

The guard didn't flinch. "I'm still gonna have to see some identification."

That cut it. Reluctantly, I fished out my wallet which told him I was not Professor Peter Collinson, I was writer Samuel Dashiell Hammett. Next thing I know I'm sitting on a very hard wooden chair looking into the very hard eyes of a six-foot three-inch cop in the interrogation room of the Beverly Hills Police Department. The giant's name was Lieutenant Etchison.

"Okay, bub," he was saying around the well-chewed stub of an unlit cigar, "what were you doing at Mr. Kelly's party?"

"Enjoying myself," I said.

He slapped me across the face with the flat of his hand. The blow made my eyes water. "Care to rephrase that answer?"

"I thought only the downtown bulls beat up the people they arrested."

"Then I guess you thought wrong," Etchison said tightly. "I'm still waiting for your answer, bub. What were you doing at Mr. Kelly's party?"

"Listening to his mother recite her lousy poetry."

He hit me again. Harder this time. With a closed fist. I could feel blood on my lip.

"I can keep doing this all night," Etchison said, rubbing his knuckles. "And by the time I'm finished it'll look like you dived head first into a meat grinder."

"Law and order in the gracious City of Beverly Hills," I said. "It's a beautiful thing."

"Whenever you're ready to quit smarting off just lemme know," said Etchison, pulling me from the chair to punch me in the stomach.

I was on my hands and knees, choking and coughing, with him leaning over me, the cigar clenched in his teeth. "Care to answer me now, wise guy?"

I struggled up to regain the chair. It wasn't an easy climb.

"Okay," I said. "I went to Kelly's to ask him for money. I figured he owed me."

"For what?"

"For a job I did on a picture he was bankrolling. I'm a writer. I did a screenplay for Kelly, but I felt I was underpaid, that I had more coming for all the work I'd put in. I was there to ask him for it."

"And what did Mr. Kelly say?"

"I never got a chance to see him. One of his security boys waylaid me and I ended up here with your fist in my mouth."

"Why the phony invitation and the fake beard—and why did you call yourself Collinson?"

"I figured I'd never get in under my own name and that this was a real good chance to see Big Bill. He's not an easy man to reach. I wasn't bothering anybody. I just wanted to see Kelly."

"Well . . . ," Etchison mused. "Maybe you're tellin' it straight."

"Then am I free to go?"

"Shit no! I'm gonna toss your rosy ass in the slammer." He grinned wickedly. "For trespassing."

Before he dragged me to a cell he used his fists on me one more time. He was good. Knew how and where to punch for maximum effect. Lieutenant Etchison was obviously enjoying himself, but it wasn't nearly as much fun for me.

Outside the cell he issued a final warning: "You tell the judge I physically abused you and I'll stick you with assault charges. Resisting arrest. Attacking an officer of the law. You won't see any daylight for a long, long time. Got that, Hammett?"

I nodded. Cut up the way I was, it was difficult to talk.

"Okay, then," he said. "I think we've reached a mutual understanding."

And he slammed the heavy cell door.

SEVENTEEN

I wasn't allowed to use the phone prior to my appearance in court the following morning. When I asked the cell guard about this (I planned to phone Buddy at the house; to him, it must have seemed that I magically "disappeared" from Kelly's party) I was refused on the grounds that B.H.P.D. prisoners were allowed just *one* call before court.

"Fine," I said. "Then take me to a phone."

"Sorry. You've already had your call," declared the guard.

"But I haven't been *near* a telephone!"

"That's not what Lieutenant Etchison told me. Says he personally saw you make your call. You care to argue with the lieutenant?"

"No, I'll pass on that."

An hour later I was standing before Judge Sinniger. He had sad eyes and flowing tufts of mustache and reminded me of an unhappy walrus.

"How do you plead to the charge of trespassing on the private property of Mr. William Kelly?"

"Guilty, Your Honor."

Then he took a closer look at me, leaning forward to peer

beneath bushy brows. "What happened to your face, Mr. Hammett?"

"I ran into an ice wagon," I told him, "and all the ice fell on me."

Judge Sinniger looked dubious, but quickly moved on to sentencing me for trespassing. I could either pay the court the sum of one hundred dollars cash—or I could spend a month in jail. Which would it be?

"I'll pay the fine, Your Honor, but naturally I don't have the money on my person at this moment."

"It is payable *now*," the walrus said.

"If you'll have your bailiff bring my wallet, the money's in there. I had exactly a hundred in cash when I was arrested last night, and you're welcome to it."

The judge consulted the papers in front of him. "Lieutenant Etchison has noted in your arrest file that when you were taken into custody your wallet contained only a single dollar bill. Are you disputing the word of Lieutenant Etchison?"

"No, no," I said. "Not at all. Obviously my memory is at fault. I'm sure that Lieutenant Etchison would not misrepresent the facts."

"Then you have no way to pay your fine?"

"Not at this precise moment, Your Honor, but if you will allow me to—"

"Thirty days!" he pronounced, rapping his gavel loudly.

I had a guard on each elbow, marching me out of the courtroom, when I heard a familiar voice behind me: "I'll pay Mr. Hammett's fine."

It was Charly to the rescue. Red-haired, befreckled Charlene Maddix, appearing in court like a ghost risen from my past to liberate me from the foul clutches of the law.

I was never so glad to see anybody in my life.

* * *

In the corner booth of MacDougall's Ice Cream Parlour, across the street from police headquarters, over a pair of double-dip strawberry sodas, I asked Charly how the devil she knew where to find me. Was she psychic?

She grinned, sucking bubble water through her straw. "I was at Kelly's party last night. I saw someone being arrested. At first I didn't know who, but when they pulled off your beard, I recognized you."

"You know Big Bill Kelly?"

"Not really," she said. "We met just once, when I was playing blackjack on his ship, but from the way he looked me over I could tell he liked what he saw. Then he told me about the lawn party for his daughter and asked if I'd like to go. I said sure and he handed me an invitation. From his standpoint, I guess you could say it was lust at first sight."

"Well, you're certainly worth lusting after."

"I'll take that as a compliment."

"How about taking it as a hint?"

Within minutes we were out of there and headed for her apartment.

"I never noticed before," I said. "You have freckles on your tummy."

"Aren't they *awful?*" Charly groaned. "I've got them all over me. Redheads have tons of freckles. Comes with the territory."

"Nice territory," I said, kissing her stomach.

We were lying on the pulldown bed in her apartment under the Gable poster and our lovemaking had been sensational. For the first time in ages I felt content, deeply at peace with myself. All thanks to Charly.

"You'll get your hundred back," I told her. "I've got money at the house."

"That cop grabbed all your cash, huh?"

"Yeah. After he finished working me over. He's a real doll, he is. Cops like Etchison make crooks look good."

I rubbed my sore jaw. I had a split on my lower lip an inch and a half long, and my face was still badly swollen. I told myself I should be thankful he hadn't used a rubber hose on me. But I guessed the lieutenant saved those for homicide investigations.

"He's probably on Kelly's payroll," said Charly.

I shrugged. "When it comes to the law around here, who isn't?"

"And you think Big Bill has the skull?"

I'd told her the whole story of the Cat's Eye—right through my plan to crack Kelly's safe.

"I'm sure he *had* it—after he iced the Greek. By now, though, it could be in Timbuktu. There's no profit for him in hanging onto the thing."

"He could break it up and sell the jewels separately. Be harder to trace that way."

"Why bother? Nobody's trying to trace it. The cops don't even know it's missing. Or care, for that matter. Besides, Kelly is smart. He knows he'll get considerably more from a private collector if he keeps the Eye intact."

"From what you've told me, a lot of people have died trying to latch onto that thing."

"Yeah, it's got quite a blood history, and just since October, five more have been added to the list: Sylvia, Tony Richetti and his son, Joe Shaw's kid, and the Greek."

"Sounds like the skull has a curse on it."

"I don't believe that crap. The news boys love to write about curses, but there's no basis to it. Pure hype to sell more papers."

"Then how do you explain all the deaths?"

"Simple. The Eye is worth a fortune and people don't mind killing each other to get it. No curse. Just human greed."

"You're a cynic, Hammett."

"I've been told that before. The truth is, I'm a realist."

"What's next? Do you have a plan?"

"I *had* a plan, and it was lousy. I got arrested before I was able to pull it off, which is probably all to the good. I might have been shot opening Kelly's safe, and getting shot is very unpleasant. I try to avoid it."

"So now what?"

"Now nothing. I'm not crazy enough to try again. It's over."

"Maybe not."

"What does that mean?"

"Maybe I could find out if Kelly still has the Cat's Eye. It's a real long shot, but I'm willing to try."

"And just what would you do?"

"I don't know exactly. But I could try."

"Stay away from Kelly. The guy's a tiger shark. He chomps up little girls like you for breakfast."

"I'm no little girl—in case you haven't noticed."

"Sure, I know, you're tougher than Joe Louis. But hear me, Charly! Keep clear of this guy. I don't want you getting hurt."

"You like me, huh?"

"Haven't I proved it?"

"Prove it again."

And her green eyes glowed.

Chandler and Gardner were waiting for me when Charly dropped me off at the Palisades house. I'd phoned Buddy from her apartment to explain my sudden disappearance and assure him that everything was jake. After my call, Gardner had phoned the house, worried that I hadn't been in touch. Buddy told him I'd be home that afternoon, so Gardner called Chandler and they came over.

The three of us sat down in the library. They didn't like the way my face looked.

179

"One of the muscled minions of the law in Beverly Hills exercised his knuckles on me," I said. "I'll be fine once the swelling's gone."

"Did they lock you up?" Erle wanted to know.

"Yeah. I spent last night in a cell with a pet cockroach. I called him Bill. In honor of Kelly."

"Thought they kept everything squeaky clean in Beverly Hills," said Ray.

"Oh, they do. Bill was a very *clean* cockroach."

"Who got you out?" asked Erle.

"A redhead with freckles," I said. "She paid my fine."

Ray grinned. "Do we know her?"

"Nope," I said. "Name's Charly Maddix, short for Charlene. I filled her in on Kelly and the Cat's Eye. Says she wants to help us get it back, but I told her to forget it, there was no way to reach Kelly."

"It's like we're all on a merry-go-round," said Erle. "We keep arriving back where we started."

"I'm sure Joe himself would tell us to give it up at this stage," said Ray.

"He doesn't even know we've been trying," I said.

"Do you think the Maddix girl is serious?" asked Erle. "About getting to Kelly, I mean."

I looked at them both. "I hope not."

But Charly *was* serious.

I found that out when I dropped by her apartment the next day. There was an envelope tacked to the front door with my name on it. Inside, a letter.

Dearest Dash,

I hope you won't be angry with me, but I have to see what I can find out about Bill Kelly and the skull.

180

Probably I won't be able to find out anything, but I'm determined to try. I'm a stubborn girl, you see! I know you wanted me to stay away from Kelly, and I really understand your concern, but I *have* to do this. I promise not to get myself into any kind of danger. I'll be out of touch for awhile—away from my apartment—but I'll phone you soon as I get back. Please, Dash, DON'T worry about me. I'm tougher than Joe Louis, remember?

Love,

Charly

All that day I tried to figure out what to do. Should I go out to the *Horseshoe* and demand to see Charly? But maybe she was somewhere else. Even if she *was* aboard Kelly's ship, why should he admit it? And if I did manage to find her, what would I do—drag her bodily back to shore? After all, Charly had a right to be where she wanted to be. What she chose to do was really none of my business. I could only hope that she'd have enough sense to stay out of trouble. I'd keep my fingers crossed.

The next morning Buddy drove me over to M-G-M in Culver City. Hunt Stromberg's assistant, a guy named Lou Prosser, was having himself a conniption fit over what he termed "monumental plot problems" on my *Thin Man* sequel. Stromberg was producer on the series but he wasn't available for this emergency story conference. Out of town, Prosser told me. In Africa somewhere. This was urgent, Prosser said. Could I be there by 10 A.M.?

As Lou phrased it: "We desperately need your creative input."

Promptly at ten, I walked into Prosser's office at M-G-M. He sat behind a desk shaped like a giant kidney. The desk, not

Prosser. Lou was skinny, like me, with a long bony nose and melancholy eyes. His hair was thinning and he combed it sideways across his high-domed forehead in an attempt to disguise the loss.

He was in sports gear: a white pullover with his name stitched across one pocket and duck-white tennis shorts. His legs were long and hairy; he also had very knobby knees.

"I was playing doubles with John Barrymore and two of the Marx brothers this morning," he said, sliding around the desk to shake my hand. "John kept stopping to swig from his gin flask, which slowed the game some."

"I hear he's doing Mercutio in *Romeo and Juliet*."

"Yep, when they can keep him sober. They're shooting the picture right here at M-G-M. Spending over two million on it. Can you believe that?"

"Lot of money," I said.

"Norma Shearer is fluttering her eyelashes as Juliet—and if you ask me, she's *way* over the hill for the role. My God, the woman must be at least thirty-five—and Shakespeare's Juliet is *fourteen!* It's a travesty."

"Yeah, I'd say she's a little long in the tooth for Juliet."

"Thalberg is producing, and Norma's *his* wife, so nobody can say a damn word about it."

Irving Thalberg was M-G-M's Boy Wonder, and his new *Mutiny on the Bounty*, with Gable and Laughton, was hot stuff. I'd met Irving once, when he visited the *Thin Man* set. He had looked bored and distracted.

"Anyhow, thanks to Barrymore and his gin flask, I didn't have time to change. Hope you can forgive the way I'm dressed."

"Hey, Lou, it'd be oke with me if you were wearing polka-dot pajamas and mink ear muffs," I told him. "I'm not here to rate your wardrobe."

"Right, right," he said briskly. "Let's us sit down and get to work on *After the Thin Man*."

"Is that what you're calling it?" I asked, settling into the office couch.

"Yes, we think it's an extremely clever title," he said, taking a chair facing me. "Has a kind of *double* meaning."

"How so?"

"Well, in a sequential sense, our picture is obviously coming 'after' the first *Thin Man,* and there's also the connotation that certain unsavory characters might be 'after' Nick Charles. You see?"

"Extremely clever," I said.

He was now consulting the screen outline I'd turned in the previous September in which I'd plotted out the full sequel. Many of my pages were paper-clipped.

"I've got notes here on a lot of sequences," he told me. "But I see no advantage in going through them page by page."

"Fine. Then what *do* you propose?"

"I need your expertise on several vexing plot points. We are literally at wit's end on them."

"Go ahead."

"Ah . . . first of all, to achieve an emotional link with the working class, Mr. Stromberg would like to change the character of Pedro Dominges from the owner of the building to the janitor."

I shrugged. "Fine."

"Then, dealing with this same character, Mr. Stromberg would like to omit the murder of Pedro which you have in your beginning. That is to say, Mr. Stromberg still wants to have him murdered, but not right there in the beginning where you have it."

"Fine," I said.

"Next, Mr. Stromberg wants Nick to get into a gun fight with Dancer when Nick goes to Polly's apartment to inspect it after Robert's murder. Dancer runs through the basement, with Nick chasing him, only they can't see each other in the dark—and *that's* when Nick finds Pedro's dead body stuffed inside a trunk, right there in the basement."

"Fine," I said.

"Then, at the climax, Mr. Stromberg doesn't want the killer to dangle Nora out of the window, threatening to drop her, the way you have it happening. Mr. Stromberg feels that the killer should, instead, hold a gun to her head. Of course, we realize that this type of ending has been done in many crime films, with the killer holding his victim at gun point, yet Mr. Stromberg finds this a more comfortable way to—"

"Fine," I said.

"Also, in this sequence, Mr. Stromberg *still* wants to have Lum Kee save Nora's life, but now we have Kee throw a hat in the killer's face and this momentary distraction results in the gun being forced from his hand."

"Fine," I said.

Lou stood up, smiling. He put the outline back on his kid-ney-shaped desk and rubbed his hands briskly together. "Well, then, that's it, Dash. I would say that our meeting today has been quite rewarding. We've accomplished a great deal in terms of action and clarity. The story line, as it now stands, is significantly improved. I'm sure that Mr. Stromberg will appreciate your coming over here on such short notice to thrash all this out."

"I'm sure he will," I said, standing up from the couch. "Is there anything else I can do for you, Lou?"

"Not a thing, Dash, not a thing." He was beaming. "I thank you most sincerely for lending your invaluable help and author's expertise in dealing with these vexing problems."

"My pleasure," I said. "Call me anytime you get vexed."

His face lit up in a megawatt smile. "You're a pip, Hammett, you really are!"

I waved to him as I walked out the door.

As Buddy drove me back to the Palisades I thought about Nick and Nora—and Hammett and Hollywood.

A hell of a way for a grown man to make a living.

EIGHTEEN

Two days went by without a word from Charly. I was starting to get the jitters, wondering if Kelly had harmed her, when the phone rang.

"Dash, it's me. Glad I caught you at home."

"I've been waiting for your call. Where are you?"

"At the Derby. In the bar."

"Did you find out anything about the Cat's Eye?"

"Just that Kelly doesn't have it."

"You mean, he's sold it?"

"No, he never had the skull in the first place. I'll explain everything when I see you. Can you come here?"

"Sure, no problem."

And I rang off. The original Brown Derby—which is shaped like one—is across from the Ambassador Hotel and Buddy got me there with no wasted time. I told him not to wait: Charly could drive me back home.

She was inside, at one of the plush leather booths. It was mid-afternoon, the slow time of day, with the lunch crowd long gone and the dinner crowd hours away. We practically had the bar to ourselves. I ordered a ginger ale and Charly was already sipping a whisky sour.

I was glad to see her and I let her know it. I'd been worried.

"But I told you *not* to," she said.

"I have a license to worry. It's one of the things I do best."

"Well, I'm sitting here with no bullet holes in me and as far as Bill Kelly is concerned, I'm virgo intacto."

"Meaning you didn't go to bed with him."

She nodded. "Not that he didn't give it the old college try. I swear, the guy must have at least eight hands."

"Start from the beginning and tell me everything."

"First, I get a kiss."

I gave her one. Charly has great lips, full and soft.

"Now, Miss Maddix," I said. "Are you ready to talk, or should I bring in my pal Lieutenant Etchison to loosen your tongue?"

"That won't sound quite so funny when I tell you what I know," she said.

"So tell me."

"On the day you got my letter I was already on board the *Horseshoe*, into some table action. I knew that Kelly would spot me and I was right. By this time he figured I liked him and that I was ripe for a tumble in the hay. We had dinner in his private cabin. During the meal he was a perfect gentleman, but after his bodyguards left he was all over me like a sex-crazed gorilla."

"But you fought him off?"

She smiled. "I didn't have to. I told him, shyly, that it was 'that time of the month' for me, and he backed away fast. A lot of men are like that."

"Smart," I said. "Real smart. What happened next?"

"He invited me to a beach party at his house in Malibu."

"Didn't know he *had* a house in Malibu."

"It's new. Custom-built for him. They just finished it last month. Kelly is wild about the place. Swims in the ocean every morning first thing after breakfast. Says it tones his system."

"So you went to the party?"

She nodded. "He even bought me a new dress for it. I looked real peachy."

"And?"

"And that's when I found out that Kelly never had the skull and doesn't have it yet."

"Yet?"

"Give me a minute and I'll get to that part. First I have to tell you about how I obtained all my inside info."

"From Kelly?"

"Nope. From one of his bodyguards, a bruiser named Happy Carter. Don't know where he got the name because he *never* smiles. Anyhow, I was doing some impressive flirting with Carter and during the party we got real chummy. He suggested a moonlight walk along the beach, which was when he began telling me the inside dope."

"About the Eye?"

"Not right away. First he tells me how much he hates Kelly and that he plans to leave him and head up to San Francisco and how would I like to go up there with him? I said I'd think it over but that I'd never met a man like him before. We were walking real close, holding hands, and it was really romantic with the full moon in the sky, the surf rolling in and all. By then he was really hooked. Women know how to pull off this kind of thing when they want to. Female instinct."

"How did you work around to the skull?"

"I didn't. Carter was telling me why he hated Kelly—that he'd done a lot of things in life that he wasn't proud of, but that he just couldn't go on working for anybody who would torture a woman."

"That's a new wrinkle," I said. "What woman was Carter talking about?"

"He didn't say. Not her name, I mean. But he *did* say that Kelly has her locked in the guest room there at the beach house and that he's been using some ugly methods in trying to pry information out of her."

"What kind of information?"

"About what Carter called 'a stolen treasure.' Apparently, Kelly thinks that the girl knows where it is."

"The Cat's Eye!"

"Exactly. Which means Kelly *didn't* get it from the Greek."

"Can you describe the woman Kelly's holding?"

"Carter doesn't know her name, but he says she's a blonde, about five four, with a trim figure. He says she's got a small mole on her left cheek."

I stared at Charly. "My God, it's the girl we saved at Big Bear—it's Jean Adams!"

After Charly dropped me off at the house I phoned Ray and Erle, telling them we were facing an emergency and it was vital that we meet right away. They both agreed; Ray would drive his Duesy to Erle's house and I'd have Buddy take me over there.

On the way, Buddy noticed how solemn I was. For most of the ride I was staring out the window, but I wasn't seeing the trees or the traffic: I was seeing the face of Jean Adams. A terrified, tortured face.

"What's wrong, Chief?" Buddy asked me. "You look spooked."

"I'll be fine," I told him. "It's nothing I want to talk about. Just get me to Erle's."

"Are you sure there isn't anything you want to tell me?"

"Not now, there isn't. Just drive, Buddy. Please."

"You got it, Chief."

And we made it to Gardner's place in record time.

Erle didn't want us to talk in the house, afraid that his Filipino houseboy might overhear the conversation. Ray was already there when I arrived, so the three of us walked out back to Erle's trailer. It was still jammed with sports equipment but we managed to find enough space to sit down. We were after privacy, not comfort.

Once we were settled I said: "I wasn't kidding about the emergency. This is very serious."

I filled them in on everything Charly had told me, as their faces reflected their deep concern.

Ray was the first to react: "Christ, Dash, we can't let Kelly get away with this! How did he get his hands on Jean Adams in the first place? You said she went back to Minnesota."

"That's what I understood from the letter she left me. But I guess she changed her mind."

"And went back to Julio?" asked Erle. "Even after he'd tried to kill her?"

"People do dumb things," I said. "Especially if they're obsessed, and maybe Jean was obsessed with Julio Richetti."

"So once they were back together again, all was forgiven, eh?" asked Ray.

"Maybe."

"Only about then Kelly discovered that Julio had turned the skull over to Papadopoulos," Erle said.

I nodded. "Yeah. Erb Yellin could have told him."

"So he kills the Greek to get it, only the Eye's not there. Julio's taken it back."

I nodded again. "Maybe he didn't like the way Papa was shooting off his mouth about the upcoming sale and decided he could do better somewhere else."

"Next," Ray put in, "Kelly finds Julio with the Adams girl, grabs her and hangs him, making it look like suicide."

"*After* planting his gun for the frame," I added.

Erle wanted to know how Kelly got one of Julio's prize guns and I said that would have been a cinch with Richetti keeping his collection on board his father's ship. Kelly could easily have lifted one of the weapons.

Erle said: "So now Kelly has Jean Adams, but he still doesn't have the Cat's Eye. He figures she knows where Julio stashed it and that she'll tell him, so Kelly begins putting the screws to her."

"That's how it is," I said. "She's a captive at his beach house right now."

Chandler nodded. There was a cold light in his eyes. "If we hadn't saved her life at Big Bear she wouldn't be in Kelly's hands."

"So what do we do about it?" Erle asked.

I looked hard at them both. "We go get her."

NINETEEN

What we were doing that night was extremely dangerous, but we had no choice. We couldn't allow Kelly to go on torturing Jean Adams—and calling in the law wouldn't help. By the time they got there, with their sirens and flashing lights, Kelly would have plenty of warning. They'd never find the girl. That is, *if* the cops responded at all; probably they wouldn't. In any case, calling them was useless.

That left us to do the job—three writers against Big Bill Kelly and his professional hoods. And on his own terrain. The odds didn't give me a lot of confidence, but when a thing has to be done, you just shut up and do it.

I was packing my .38 and Gardner had his bow and arrows. Even Chandler was armed—with an antique sword cane he'd bought in London back when he was in school over there. He never figured he'd be using it to rescue damsels in distress. We hadn't done such a great job in our first such attempt—the night we tried to rescue Clare from Tony Richetti. She was dead when we got to her, which I hoped wouldn't be the case with Jean Adams.

Thanks to Charly, we knew exactly where we were going as

well as the basic layout of the house. At least the weather was on our side. A damp coastal fog was rolling in from the Pacific and would give us some cover at the beach.

I knew that Kelly always had four bodyguards with him and I remembered their impassive faces from my visit to the *Horseshoe*. Happy Carter would be among them, unless he'd walked off the job by now. But from the way Charly talked, he was wasn't cutting out for Frisco until next week.

We were in Chandler's big Duesy with the top up to avoid the night chill. Ray was driving and he looked nervous, but then we were all nervous.

"Are we going to have to kill anybody?" Gardner asked me.

"Possibly," I said. "I'd like to avoid it, but we'll never be able to reach the girl until Kelly and his boys are put out of business."

"This is really insane," said Ray, as the Duesy's big fog light sliced through the white mist ahead of us. *"We're the ones who could get killed!"*

"That's possible, too," I said.

The fog thickened as we approached Malibu. Just beyond the coast highway I could hear the deep rumble of ocean, like an unseen giant breathing heavily in the darkness. Usually, the Pacific exerts a calming effect on me, but not now; on this particular night the ocean sounded ominous and threatening.

"Slow down," I told Ray. "The house should be less than half a mile from here. Charly said to look for a Richfield station on the side opposite the beach. We can park there."

"I feel as if I'm back in the war," said Chandler. "And I don't like it."

"There's the gas station," said Erle. "Ahead on the right."

The place was closed so we were able to park behind one of the pumps. The fog swirled around us as we got out of the car. I turned up my coat collar to ward off the sharp night chill. The loaded .38 under my left armpit felt warm and solid in its holster. I hoped I wouldn't have to kill anybody with it.

"We'll come in from the ocean," I said. "That's the best way to reach Kelly's house."

Gardner had a bow slung over one shoulder along with several metal-tipped arrows in a leather carrying case, and Chandler gripped his Malacca sword cane as we scrambled down a flight of badly weathered wooden steps leading to the beach.

The sand mounded under our shoes; it was like walking through thick mud. Relentlessly, the ocean swept in, spreading its white curls across the beach as it has been doing now for the past million-plus years, not giving a damn about kidnapped girls or jeweled skulls.

Kelly's house was easy to spot, being the only one with a wooden tower rising a full story above the second-floor roof. Charly claimed that Big Bill had it built for the view, but I think he did it because it made him feel like a king. It contained a study and a guest bedroom, which was where Jean Adams was being held. She was the captive blonde princess in the tower and we were an unlikely trio of knights bent on rescue. One of us even had a sword!

Suddenly I felt Erle grip my arm, pulling me down in the sand. Chandler was kneeling beside us.

"What's wrong?" I asked.

"There's a guy on the beach in front of Kelly's place," Erle told me. "Near the water."

On a cold night like this I hadn't expected to encounter any of Big Bill's crew outside the house—but this was definitely a Kelly man. I recognized him as he lit a cigarette, the match flaring against his cupped hands. He was one of the bodyguards I'd seen aboard the *Horseshoe*. He might even be Happy Carter.

"Can we grab him?" asked Ray.

I shook my head. "There's too much open sand. He'd see us coming, even in the fog. You'll have to use your bow."

"I think I can put one in his shoulder," Erle said.

Ray looked worried. "Won't he let out a yell?"

"Nobody at the house can hear him even if he does," said Erle. "Not with the sound of the ocean."

"Yeah," I said. "Once he's hit, we can rush him."

"Okay, then," nodded Erle. "Here goes."

He notched an arrow into the bow, drew it back taut, and let fly. Perfect shot. The guy yelped like a stepped-on puppy, falling into the sand and clutching at his left shoulder.

He was groaning loudly when Ray put him to sleep with a sharp blow from his cane. "One down," he grinned. I think he was beginning to enjoy himself.

The fog-muffled roar of a heavy weapon spun me around. I saw a crouching figure maybe thirty feet down the beach coming toward us with a .45 in his hand.

"Christ!" gasped Chandler, who had thrown himself into the damp sand. "That bullet almost got me!" And he held out his right arm, displaying a neat hole through the sleeve of his coat.

Erle slithered up to us on his stomach. "Lights are going on all over the house! We're cooked meat!"

"Not yet we aren't," I said, pulling my .38 from its holster. The fog was patchy, with broken stretches of visibility. When I had a clear view I drew a bead on the advancing gunman. He was approaching cautiously, the .45 up and ready.

I fired and he went down. Had I killed him? There was no time to wonder about it.

"C'mon," I yelled. "Let's move!"

The old cliché was true: offense is often the best defense—and the three of us charged straight for the house.

There was a spatter of gunfire ahead of us. Big Bill's other two bodyguards were on the outside deck, firing blindly into the fog. With the house lights at their back, they made prime targets. Erle took out the first with an arrow in the thigh while I dispatched the second with a .38 round in the kneecap. They went down like cut timber.

Reaching the deck, I disarmed the two of them, tossing their guns into the darkness. They were both in a state of shock, but they weren't my concern right then. Kelly was.

"Where is he?" I demanded of the guy with the shattered kneecap. "Where's your boss?"

"Tower . . ." he gasped, holding his leg, face drained of color. "When the fireworks started . . . Kelly headed for the tower."

I leaned closer to him. "How many others in the house?"

"Nobody . . . I mean, just Kelly and the dame."

"Jean Adams?"

"I guess that's her name . . . a blonde."

"You two wait here," I said to Erle and Ray. "I'm going in after Kelly."

"We'll go with you," said Erle.

"Right," Ray nodded.

"No, *I'm* the one with the gun—and Kelly is armed. This is my job."

As Ray started to protest I raised a silencing hand. No one would be going in after Kelly—he was coming out to us.

Big Bill stepped through the sliding-glass doorway with Jean Adams in front of him. He had a Browning automatic pressed against the side of her head. Her face was worse than I'd imagined—battered and bruised, her eyes puffed and swollen, scabs on her lips. She'd taken a lot from him.

"Lose the .38," Big Bill said to me. I let it drop.

"Now kick it away."

I did that. It slid off the edge of the deck, falling into the sand.

"Toss the bow," he said to Gardner, who obeyed without hesitation. The glitter in Kelly's eyes told us he was ready to trigger the Browning if anyone crossed him.

"Now, you boys are going to stay right here while I walk the girl out to my car. We get in and I drive away. At that point, you can do whatever you damn well please."

He nodded toward his two groaning bodyguards, who were lying on the deck. "Some shitty pair you are!" he said in contempt.

"They hurt us, boss," complained the one I'd shot.

"I'm sorry they didn't kill you," growled Kelly.

He turned to us: "Maybe you're wondering why I don't just waste the three of you here and now."

"I'm sure you have a reason," I said.

"It amuses me to let you live," Kelly declared. "I want each of you to savor your failure here tonight. Once I get what I'm after from the girl, she'll end up at the bottom of the Pacific, and you won't have a shred of evidence against me. Think about it, boys. Think about what a trio of hopeless fuck-ups you are."

And, laughing, he nudged Jean back inside, keeping the gun to her head. We watched him cross the living room to a side door which led to his parked car. "Adios, suckers!"

The instant the door closed, Ray lunged forward, his sword cane unsheathed. I grabbed his coat and yanked him back.

"Let me go!" he shouted. "I've got this!"

"And he's got a Browning automatic. Don't be a sap, Ray. It's no contest. Stick your head through that door and he'll blast it off."

We heard the sound of a starter.

Then, abruptly, we heard four shots, closely spaced, like sharp handclaps.

"He's killed her!" Erle exclaimed.

We were halfway across the living room and moving for the door when it opened. Jean was there, clutching the automatic in her right hand. She staggered into the room, dropping into a chair by the fireplace. "I finished him," she said softly, her eyes closed. "I killed the bastard."

I walked over to her, flanked by Ray and Erle, extending my right hand. "Give it to me."

Numbly, she passed over the Browning.

"How'd you manage it?" I asked her.

"He . . . he got distracted when he was starting the car," she said in a low voice. "I was able to grab the gun."

"You sure he's dead?" Ray asked.

She nodded.

"He had it coming," said Erle. "He sure as hell had it coming."

She looked at us, tears in her eyes. "Kelly was behind everything. Once he discovered that Tony Richetti had the Cat's Eye, he killed him to get it, but Julio outsmarted him and got away clean with the skull. I was certain Julio had done the killings, and he knew he could never convince me he hadn't. That's why he decided to get rid of me at the lodge. When I tried to go back to Minnesota, Kelly had me followed. He thought I knew where Julio had taken the Cat's Eye, but I didn't. I *swore* to him I didn't know where it was, but he wouldn't believe me. He . . . he did . . . terrible things to me."

She held out her right arm. It was red and there were raw wounds; cigarettes had seared the flesh.

"That lousy son of a bitch," muttered Chandler.

"There's just one thing about all this that continues to bother me," I said. "Why would Kelly kill Clare Vanikis?"

"Tony used her to get the skull from Joe Shaw," said Jean. "Kelly didn't give a damn about her. She was just in his way."

"The papers said that a young woman named Mae Tilford was among the passengers lost at sea that night," I said to Jean. "It was assumed she jumped from the *Lady* to avoid the fire, but her body was never recovered. Did you know her?"

Jean shook her head. "I never heard the name until now."

"I did some checking and found out that she'd been working

for Tony Richetti as a hostess aboard the *Lady*. Dark-haired, about twenty, and single. What if Mae Tilford was the woman found dead in Tony's cabin that night with Clare's ring on her finger? The bullets blew most of her face away, so her family wouldn't have been able to recognize her even if they'd been shown the body."

Jean stared at me. "Are you saying that you think someone substituted Mae Tilford for Clare Vanikis?"

"It *could* have been done. Clare had dark hair and so did Mae, and the age was right. With Clare's ring on her finger, and Clare's ID in her purse, she was a perfect ringer."

Jean looked confused. "But why would anyone do such a thing? For what purpose?"

"To make it appear that Clare Vanikis was dead, enabling the *real* Clare to run off with Julio and fence the Cat's Eye." I looked steadily into her brown eyes. "And you almost pulled it off."

There was an audible gasp from Chandler—and Erle wore a stunned look.

"You're crazy!" the girl declared. "Your whole story is crazy! What makes you think I'm Clare Vanikis?"

"I wasn't sure until tonight. But I had a gut hunch that something about 'Jean Adams' was phony. I couldn't pin it down until tonight . . . until I got a close look at your hair."

"My *hair*! That's crazy, too. Clare was a *brunette*, for God's sake! I'm a blonde."

"Not really," I said. "Since Kelly grabbed you, there's been no chance for you to get a bleach." I ran my hand along her head. "Your roots are showing, Clare."

That's when she made a grab for the Browning, throwing herself out of the chair at me. She raked my forehead with her nails as we struggled for possession of the gun. Blood welled into my eyes and I almost lost my grip on the automatic. Until Chandler pulled her away from me.

He slammed her onto the couch. "You murdering little bitch! I wish to Christ we'd never saved your miserable life!"

She seemed suddenly drained of strength, slumping back weakly against the cushions. Her breathing was fast and shallow. Finally, she looked up at the three of us standing over her.

"Sit down, boys," she said, "and I'll tell you all about it."

TWENTY

I kept the gun leveled on Clare as she spun out her confession. I remember how easily the words flowed—as if she had been waiting all this time to tell her story. It was a dark and disturbing one, going all the way back to her childhood in West Virginia.

"I was badly mistreated by the people who raised me," she said. "They worked me like a farm hand and beat me constantly, to get the Devil out of my soul, they said. And the man—he started *touching* me the first night I was there, when I was six. After that, it just got worse. A year later, when I was seven, he started having intercourse with me. I hated him more than you'll ever know. When I told his wife what he was doing, she said to get used to it, that's what God made girls for and it was going to happen to me all the rest of my life. I think she was happy about it because, when her husband was with me, he wasn't bothering her."

Erle and Ray looked shocked, but I'd heard similar stories when I was a Pinkerton. A lot of ugly things happen that never make the papers. Unfortunately, Clare's history was not unique.

"I hated school, too, which is why I left a year short of graduation," she continued. "I was full of anger at being abandoned by my mother, who became this big Hollywood star after she changed her name from Vanikis to Vane. She should have spelled it V-A-I-N because that's what she was. All she ever thought about was herself. Obviously, she never gave a damn about me. I had a horrible life and my mother just didn't care."

"Your father cared about you," I said. "Joe Shaw gave up the Cat's Eye to get you back."

"He was never anything to me," she declared. "When he sent that necklace for my eighteenth birthday, it didn't mean anything. It was like a gift from someone in a story."

"What did you do after you quit school?"

"Hitchhiked to California. I never told anybody where I was going. I needed money, so I got a job with an outfit in Hollywood called Success Unlimited. They billed themselves as a talent agency, but that was a cover. Their real business was sex. One of the things they did was to supply Tony Richetti with the women he hired for his gambling boat. Sort of glorified prostitutes. I was one of them."

"Along with Mae Tilford?"

"That's right. I got to know Mae after I went to work for Tony. We were a lot alike. Same hair, eyes, height—even the same age. Well, I was actually a year older. Mae didn't mind doing what we did, but to me it was awful—my childhood all over again. The same horrible older men, the same helpless feelings of terror, like I couldn't do anything to defend myself, to make them stop. I was looking for a way out when I met Tony's son, Julio. He took a real shine to me. Pretty soon he was crazy in love."

"Did you love *him*?" I asked her.

"Never. Not for a second. He was too immature and full of himself, and someday he was going to be a horrible old man. I could tell. In a few years, he was going to be just like all the others. Anyway, we got into this steamy affair, with him buying me stuff and taking me out to expensive nightclubs like the Coconut Grove and all. It was okay. Because he was Tony Richetti's son, for the first time in my life I was sort of protected. I didn't have to be with the customers anymore, so it was fine by me."

"Did your mother know you were in California?"

"No. Why should she? I hadn't seen her since she'd dumped me when I was six and I didn't *want* to see her again. I used to read about her in the movie magazines because I was curious, but then I'd throw the magazines across the room."

"She might have helped you get into films. Did you ever think about that?"

"Sure, I thought about it. Every girl does. But I didn't want any kind of help from her. It would have turned my stomach."

I kept firing questions: "Did you ever see her on board the *Lady*? She gambled there all the time."

"Yeah, I saw her. Once I walked right up to her with a drink. She looked at me and gave me one of her phony movie star smiles. Didn't have a clue as to who I really was. She was always playing the sex queen, with the guys around her lapping it up. Then I found out that Tony was putting pressure on her to pay off a gambling debt. That gave me my idea about the Cat's Eye."

"How did you know about the Eye?"

"When I was around four or five, before Sylvia sent me to West Virginia, she used to brag about this 'family treasure.' She made it sound like something out of the Arabian Nights—this dazzling jeweled skull with its fantastic history of blood and violence that finally ended up in my father's possession. As I got older, I used to dream about the Cat's Eye, of owning it and being wealthy. Now, in California, I saw a way to turn my childhood fairy-tale into reality. All the elements were in place. They just needed to be used."

"Was Tony Richetti aware of the skull?"

"No, not at all. I didn't tell anybody about it. The first thing I had to do was learn to imitate Tony's handwriting. I'd practice for hours every day, doing his loops and curls and crossing t's like he did. I got so my writing could easily pass for his. After that, I killed Sylvia with a knife. Made it look as if Tony had done it."

"How could you murder your own mother?"

"It was easy. I just remembered how she left me in West Virginia with those horrible people and it was easy. She *deserved* to die for what she did to me."

It took a moment to get past the coldness of Clare's words. I had a flashback image of Sylvia, lying on that tiled hallway floor in a spreading pool of her own blood. Then I blinked away the memory. "So you wrote the letter to your father, Joe Shaw—the letter I told him came from Tony Richetti?"

"Yes—and I sent along the silver necklace to convince him. He knew that unless he turned over the Cat's Eye as ransom he'd never see his only child again. I guess that's when you came into it."

"When I got slugged at the train station in Pasadena, *you* were the one who sapped me?"

"Uh-huh. And I just waltzed right out of there with the Cat's Eye." She smiled impishly.

"What about the fire on board the *Lady*? Was that your doing, too?

"Julio helped me start it, as a diversion. Then I gunned down Tony and Mae. I set it up so she had my purse and ring to make it look like poor Clare had been killed along with Richetti. After that, I bleached my hair and became Jean Adams."

"Why did you involve Julio? You didn't have to."

"Because he had this connection with Papadopoulos. Julio was sure the Greek could make a great sale on the Eye, so I let him fence it. I told him we'd split the take, fifty-fifty, after the Greek's cut."

"You intended giving Julio half of what you got?"

"God, no! I was just using him to get the Eye sold at the best price. Once we had the money, I was going to kill him."

It passed through my mind that Joe's daughter could have taught Brigid O'Shaughnessy a few things.

"What happened up at Big Bear? Did Julio really try to set you up as a suicide?"

"Oh, yeah. Yeah. That was a close one. It started with an argument between us. By then the Greek had the skull and was blabbing to anyone who'd listen about this 'treasure' he was going to unload. I told Julio we had to get the skull back and take it somewhere else, but he said no, that everything was set for the deal that was coming up in just a few days. He didn't want to switch horses in midstream."

"I can see his point."

"Well, I couldn't. We got into a terrible row, with Julio yelling that I'd become a liability to him and that with me out of the way he'd have all the dough for himself."

"Not knowing that was exactly what *you* planned for him."

"Ironic, huh?" She smiled. "Anyway, he forced me to swallow some sleeping powder. After I was out cold, he arranged the scene in the garage. I would have died in that place if the three of you hadn't come along when you did."

"You were good," I said. "I bought your little-girl-from-Minnesota routine."

"We *all* did," admitted Erle.

"I wish we hadn't bothered to save you," said Ray coldly. "You didn't deserve to live."

Clare shrugged. "After I left you guys, I wrote that tearjerking letter about having to go back home to Minnesota. Then I drove out to see the Greek. I'd taken along one of Julio's fancy guns and I used it on Papadopoulos after I got him to open the safe."

"Which had the Eye inside?"

"Right. I took it away with me. Then I went to Julio's apartment. I set up the hanging to make it look like he'd killed himself. In other words, I did to him what he tried to do to me. Poetic justice."

"How did you get him up there? Physically, how did you do it?"

"I held the gun on him," she said, "and he did exactly what I told him to do. He knew I'd shoot if he didn't. I had him climb on a chair with the cord around his neck. Then I had him tie the other end to an overhead pipe. He was begging me to let him go. He kept saying 'I know you don't really want to do this.' He thought he could sweet-talk me out of it. When I kicked the chair away and left him dangling, the expression on his face was priceless. His eyes bugged way out and I heard his neck snap. I'd never seen anything like it before. It was really interesting."

I let her words sink in for a moment and then I asked: "And you were the one who sent the note and put in that anonymous call to the police?"

"Sure, after I left Julio's gun in a trash barrel behind the Greek's shop so the cops could find it. It all worked like a charm. What I *didn't* know was that word had reached Bill Kelly about the Cat's Eye and he was having me followed. They grabbed me when I left Julio's apartment."

"You didn't have the skull with you?"

"Hell, no! I'm not stupid. I stashed it in a safe place before I went over to deal with lover boy."

"Then Kelly had you brought out here to Malibu."

"Yeah. And he was *rough*. He began working me over to find out where the Eye was, but I didn't break. I never told him a damn thing."

"I have a question," said Chandler. "At the train station in Pasadena, after you sapped Hammett, you had a clear run with the skull. Why didn't you just leave town? Why stick around to set up the ship killings and all the rest of it? You were free as a bird. Nobody could have traced you."

206

"I had some scores to settle," she said grimly. "When I first went to work on the *Lady*, Tony arranged a private party in his cabin. Kelly was there as a guest and Richetti just handed me over to him the way you'd hand somebody a drink. What happened after that was a nightmare. Bill Kelly was a sadist, a depraved sex pervert, worse than any man I'd ever been with before. He almost killed me! I promised myself I would get even with him somehow. When I got a chance to steal his cigarette lighter, I figured I *had* him."

"So you tried to frame Kelly for the ship murders by leaving his lighter in the cabin?"

She nodded. "But it didn't work, did it? The lighter just wasn't enough to make the frame stick. But I was finally able to pay him off tonight by putting four slugs in his rotten head." She smiled. "That was delicious!"

"First your mother," I said. "Then Tony Richetti and Mae Tilford. Then Papadopoulos and Julio. Now Bill Kelly. You've run up quite a score."

"They all deserved what they got," she said flatly.

"Even your mother?" asked Gardner.

"Her most of all. You don't just ship your kid off to another family and forget all about her so you can go be a big star in Hollywood."

"I'll admit that Kelly and the Richettis are no loss to society," said Gardner.

"So who's innocent?" Clare asked us. "The Greek was a greedy, drug-peddling loudmouth who would have conned Abe Lincoln if he'd had the chance, and Mae was nothing but a prostitute who didn't see anything wrong with what she did. It's like I said, they all deserved what they got."

"I doubt that a judge and jury will see it that way," Gardner declared.

"There's one thing you all seem to forget," Clare said. "I still

207

have the Eye and it's worth big money. You let me go, and we split the take four ways."

"First," I said, "we need to see it."

"Do we have a deal?"

"Just tell us where the skull is," I snapped. "You're in no position to bargain right now." My tone was harsh. "Where *is* it?"

"There's a locker key taped inside the right front fender of the Chrysler," she said. "You know, the one I drove away from Big Bear in."

Chandler frowned. "Where's the car now?"

"Parked on the street in front of my apartment." She gave us the address. "So—do we have a deal? Are we partners?"

I grinned at her. "I'd as soon be partners with a guttersnake." The others nodded agreement.

"You lousy bastards!" She dived past me for the door, reached it, then jumped from the outside deck to the sand, with the three of us at her heels.

The fog had thinned and Clare was easily visible in the ivory wash of moonlight. A clear target.

"You'd better shoot!" yelled Chandler. "She's going for the ocean!"

"Let her," I said, watching the running figure cross the surf line and begin swimming away from us. "She'll die out there."

"But that's just what she *wants*," Erle protested. "She's killing herself to cheat the law. It's too easy!"

He ran to the edge of the sand, stripped off his heavy jacket, and plunged into the water, stroking after her. Erle was a strong, fast swimmer.

Ten minutes later he carried her into the house. She looked like a drowned rat, her hair tangled with sand and seaweed, eyes closed, totally exhausted after her struggle with Gardner.

"I still think she rated a bullet," said Chandler softly. I was surprised to hear him say it, as much as he hated guns.

Erle shook his head. "She'll get worse than a bullet for what she's done."

I couldn't argue with that.

We turned Clare over to the cops. The key she'd taped inside the Chrysler's fender led us straight back to the Santa Fe train station in Pasadena. We drove there in Ray's Duesy. He and Erle were like a couple of excited kids; they could hardly wait to have a gander at the Cat's Eye.

"Why would she take it back to Pasadena?" Ray wanted to know. "That's where she grabbed it in the first place."

"Which means nobody would ever be looking for it there," I said.

"Smart," agreed Erle. "Real smart. She had every angle figured."

"Except Big Bill," I said. "Clare never figured on being kidnapped by Kelly before she could get back to the Eye."

When I keyed open the locker I was nervous. I wasn't even sure the skull would be inside. But it was. Wrapped in coarse brown paper. I took it from the shelf and handed it to Chandler.

"You do the honors," I said.

Ray carefully unwrapped the treasure, with Erle leaning forward in close attendance.

And there it was. The Cat's Eye. Chandler held it into the light and its faceted jewels became points of dancing fire in the shaft of sun which streamed in from the station window.

"Wow!" breathed Chandler.

"I can understand why so many people have been killed over this," declared Gardner. "It's really something."

"Yeah," I said, "something I'll be damn glad to hand over to Joe Shaw. I'm taking it back to him."

But before I did, I had dinner with Charly at the Derby. We talked about the beach fracas in Malibu. None of Kelly's bodyguards had been killed, but two of them were in the hospital.

Charly said she wanted to go with me to New York on the train. A romantic cross-country trip and all that.

"Nix," I said. "This job isn't finished until I've handed the skull over to Shaw. When I get back, there'll be plenty of time for the two of us."

"I'll count on that," she said, pressing my hand.

Even though I'd phoned Joe about Clare and the skull, he was still not emotionally prepared to see me.

The news about his daughter had rocked him; he couldn't believe she'd turned out the way she had and he blamed himself.

We were in his office in New York, with the skull facing us on his desk, when he told me how guilty he felt.

"I didn't know how to act like a father," he said darkly. "I didn't even *try*. If I'd tried, I could have changed things."

"How?" I asked.

"I could have reached Clare through Sylvia. She knew where my daughter was. I should have forced her to tell me. That family who had her in West Virginia—those monsters who mistreated her—I could have taken Clare away from them. Maybe sent her to boarding school or something."

"Then why didn't you?"

"Because I was weak. I never accepted the responsibility of having a child. I left it all up to Sylvia, and it was absolutely wrong of me to do that. I was Clare's *father*, for Christ's sake! I should have *helped* her. If I had. . ." His head was bowed. ". . . things might have turned out a lot differently."

"At least you've hired a good attorney for her," I said.

He raised his head. "An empty gesture. Too little, too late. She'll get the death sentence. And, in a very real way, *I'll* have killed her—and all the others, too."

"You're being pretty tough on yourself."

His eyes blazed. "That's crap and you know it. In large part, *I'm* responsible for the monster my daughter turned into. And I'll have to live with that knowledge for the rest of my life. Day and night, I'll have to live with it."

He stared dully at the glittering skull on his desk. "And they all died . . . because of *this*."

"Funny thing about the Eye," I said. "Turns out it's a lot closer to my falcon that I'd imagined."

"What do you mean?"

"I worked for a diamond seller once in Frisco so I know something about jewels. After I got the Eye out of the locker in Pasadena I took my first real close look at it. That made me decide to have it appraised by a pal of mine in Beverly Hills—a real expert on stuff like this. He told me how much it's worth."

"Which is?"

"Less than a hundred bucks," I said. "Your family treasure is a fake."

Joe slumped back in his desk chair, a thin smile on his face. "And no one knew?"

"The Greek would have found out when he actually tried to sell it," I said.

"But what about its *history*? Centuries of bloodshed. People killing each other across the world to possess it. Surely all these deaths would never have happened if the Eye's worthless."

I shrugged. "Oh, I'm sure there *was* a genuine jeweled skull. But somewhere along the line somebody switched it for this fake one. Could even have been someone in your family."

"So the Cat's Eye is a fake," Shaw said. "What's real, Dash?" His eyes held a lot of pain. "Can you tell me what's real?"

"Love. Honor. Friendship. The air we breathe. The sun in the sky. A lot of things are real. We just have to learn not to depend on what isn't."

But Joe wasn't listening. He had his head down again. I knew he was thinking about Clare.

He'd be thinking about her for a long, long time.

AUTHOR'S AFTERWORD

A few necessary words.

The Black Mask Murders is the first in an extensive series of Hollywood thrillers set in the 1930s, featuring three real-life crime writers here projected as fictional crime solvers. Each will have his turn at telling the story. The initial novel is narrated by Dashiell Hammett; in *The Marble Orchard* Raymond Chandler will narrate, and in *Sharks Never Sleep* the narrator will be Erle Stanley Gardner. This alternating cycle will continue with Hammett narrating the fourth book in the series, Chandler the fifth, Gardner the sixth—and so on.

The novels will be a calculated mix of fiction and fact. Which is to say that the life history of each writer-sleuth is totally authentic, based on biographical fact, while the plots they become involved in over the course of the series are very much the stuff of fiction.

The series background is also authentic Hollywood as it existed in its Golden Age, replete with a mix of real people and fictional characters. Joseph T. Shaw was indeed the New York editor of *Black Mask* magazine in the 1930s (although Clare and Sylvia never existed)—and an actual jeweled skull *did* inspire

Hammett to write *The Maltese Falcon*. It is described, along with a color photo, in the November 1975 issue of *City of San Francisco*. I quote from an interview in the magazine with ex-Pinkerton agent Phil Haultain, who worked with Hammett in the early '20s:

> Haultain pointed to a black, jewel-encrusted object on his desk. "It's the skull of a holy man . . . once used to hold blood from human sacrifices. I keep it as a family heirloom. An uncle of mine, who lived in Calcutta, India, sent it to me. It was taken as loot by a member of the British Expedition to Lhasa, Tibet. The original owner . . . put a curse on it. . . . When *The Maltese Falcon* came out that book rang a lot of bells."

I don't need to say anything more. Hammett, Chandler, and Gardner will tell you the rest. The Black Mask Boys can speak for themselves.

Me, I'm just along for the ride.

—William F. Nolan